Gianrico Carofiglio, born in 1961, was an anti-Mafia prosecutor in the southern Italian city of Bari for many years. He has been responsible for some of the most important indictments in the region involving organized crime, corruption and the traffic in human beings. He is now a Member of the Italian Senate. *A Walk in the Dark* was the second in a series with defence lawyer Guido Guerrieri. It won numerous literary prizes and has been translated into eleven languages.

Other Bitter Lemon books featuring Guido Guerrieri

Involuntary Witness
Reasonable Doubts

A WALK IN THE DARK

Gianrico Carofiglio

Translated from the Italian
by Howard Curtis

BITTER LEMON PRESS
LONDON

BITTER LEMON PRESS

First published in the United Kingdom in 2006 by
Bitter Lemon Press, 37 Arundel Gardens, London W11 2LW
This new edition published in 2010

www.bitterlemonpress.com

First published in Italian as *Ad occhi chiusi* by
Sellerio editore, Palermo, 2003

This edition is published with the financial assistance of the Italian
Ministry of Foreign Affairs

Acknowledgements
Page 57: 'The Ghost of Tom Joad' by Bruce Springsteen. © Bruce
Springsteen. All rights reserved. Reprinted by permission. Page
167: 'Losing My Religion' Words and Music by William Berry, Peter
Buck, Mike Mills and Michael Stipe. © 1991 Night Garden Music.
Administered by Warner-Tamerlane Publishing Corp. All rights
reserved. Used by permission.

A CIP record for this book is available from the British Library

ISBN 978–1–904738–53–4

Typeset by RefineCatch Limited, Broad Street, Bungay, Suffolk

Printed and bound by Cox & Wyman Ltd, Reading, Berks

Part One

1

You never quit smoking.

You give up for a while. Days, months, years. But you never quit completely. Cigarettes are always there, lying in wait. Sometimes they appear in the middle of a dream, even five or ten years after you've "quit".

You feel the touch of the paper on your fingers, you hear the soft, dull, reassuring noise it makes when you tap it on your desk, you feel the touch of the ochre filter on your lips, you hear the scrape of the match and you see the yellow flame with its blue base.

You even feel the kick in your lungs, and you see the smoke spreading over your papers, your books, your cup of coffee.

And then you wake up. And you think a cigarette, just one cigarette, won't matter very much. You could light one right now, because you always have that emergency packet in your desk drawer, or somewhere else. And then, of course, you tell yourself it doesn't work like that, that if you light one you'll light another, and then another, and so on, and so on. Sometimes it works, sometimes it doesn't. Whatever happens, it's at moments like these that you realize the phrase "to quit smoking" is an abstract concept. The reality is quite different.

And then there are other times, more concrete than dreams. Nightmares, for example.

*

It had already been a few months since I'd stopped smoking.

I was on my way back from the Public Prosecutor's department, where I had been studying the documents relating to a civil action in which I was involved. And I had a bloody great desire to go into a tobacconist's, buy a packet of strong, sharp-tasting cigarettes – yellow MSs, maybe – and smoke them till my lungs burst.

I'd been hired by the parents of a little girl who'd been the victim of a paedophile. He'd waited outside her school, had called to her, and she'd followed him. They'd both gone into the entrance hall of an old apartment block. The woman caretaker had seen them, and had followed them in. The pervert was rubbing the flies of his trousers against the girl's face, the girl's eyes were closed and she wasn't saying anything.

The caretaker had screamed. The pervert had escaped, raising his collar as he did so. Simple but effective, because the caretaker hadn't managed to get a good look at his face.

When the girl had been questioned, with the help of a nice lady psychologist, it had emerged that this hadn't been the first time. Not even the second or third time.

The police had done their job well. They'd identified the pervert, and had photographed him secretly. Outside the council office where he worked – a model employee. The girl had recognized him. She'd pointed at the photograph, her teeth chattering, and then looked away.

When the police had gone to arrest him, they'd found a collection of photos. Photos straight out of a nightmare.

The photos I'd seen that morning, in the file.

I wanted to smash someone's face. The pervert's, if I could. Or his lawyer's. The lawyer had written that "the little girl's statements are clearly unreliable, the result of morbid fantasies typical of certain individuals at a prepubescent age". I'd really have liked to smash his face. I'd also have liked to smash the faces of the appeal court judges, who'd put the paedophile under house arrest. According to their ruling, "to avoid the risk of repetition of admittedly serious acts of the kind at issue in this case, restriction of personal freedom in the lesser form of house arrest is sufficient".

They were right. Technically, they were right. I knew that perfectly well, I was a lawyer. I myself had upheld the same principle many times. For my own clients. Thieves, con men, armed robbers, fraudulent bankrupts. Even a few drug dealers.

But not men who raped children.

Be that as it may, I wanted to smash someone's face.

Or smoke.

Or do anything rather than go back to my office to work.

2

But I did go to my office, and worked without stopping, not even to eat, until late afternoon. Then I told Maria Teresa I had something urgent to do, and escaped to a bookshop.

I stayed there, browsing, until the shop closed. I was the last to leave. The shutter was already half lowered, and the assistants were all lined up at the cash desk, looking at me in an unfriendly way.

I rang the bell of Margherita's apartment and waited for her to come and open the door.

I had keys, but almost never used them. She didn't use hers to my apartment, two floors below, either.

We'd each kept our own apartment, with our own books, posters, discs, and so on: a mess, in the case of my little apartment. Hers was a penthouse, big, beautiful and tidy. Not obsessively tidy. Tidy like the home of someone who is in perfect control of the situation. Of the two of us, she was the one in control, but that was fine by me.

The only change had been in her apartment. We'd bought a king-size bed, the largest we could find, and had put it in her bedroom. I'd taken over a corner of the wardrobe for myself and had put in a few of my things. One shelf in the bathroom was also mine. And that was it.

I often slept at her place. But not always. Sometimes

I felt like watching TV until late – though less and less – and sometimes I wanted to read until late. Sometimes she was the one who wanted to sleep alone, without anyone around. Sometimes one of us went out with friends. Sometimes she left for work and I stayed at home. I never went into her apartment when she was out. I missed her even when she'd only been gone a few hours.

I rang again just as the door opened.

"Nervous?"

"Deaf?"

"If you want to fast, you just have to say so. No point in beating about the bush."

I didn't want to fast. From inside the apartment came a nice smell of freshly cooked food. I raised my hands to my chest, palms turned outwards as a sign of surrender, and squeezed past her to get inside.

"Did I tell you you could come in?"

"I bought you a book."

She looked at my empty hands, and I took the bookshop bag from the pocket of my winter jacket. Then she closed the door.

"What is it?"

"Constantin Cavafy. A Greek poet. Listen to this. It's called 'Ithaca'."

I opened the white book, sat down on the sofa, and read:

> *Hope that the way is long,*
> *That the summer mornings are many,*
> *When you enter at last, with such joy,*
> *Ports you are seeing for the first time:*
> *May you stop at Phoenician markets*
> *And purchase fine goods,*
> *Mother-of-pearl and coral, amber and ebony,*

> *And sensual perfumes of every kind,*
> *As many sensual perfumes as you can,*
> *And may you visit many Egyptian cities*
> *To learn and learn from their scholars*
> *Always keep Ithaca in your mind*
> *To arrive there is your destiny.*
> *But do not hurry the journey in any way.*
> *Better that it should last for years . . .*

Margherita took the book out of my hands. Keeping the place with her finger, she looked at the cover – there was no illustration on it, just a poem – passed her finger over the smooth white paper, and read the back page. Then she turned back to the poem I'd been reading and I saw she was moving her lips, silently.

When she'd finished, she looked at me and gave me a quick kiss.

"OK. You can stay and eat. Wash your hands, put a CD on and lay the table. In that order."

I washed my hands. I put on Tracy Chapman. I laid the table and poured myself a glass of wine. I still wanted a cigarette but, at least for today, the worst was over.

3

After dinner, we both felt like going out. We decided to go to a venue that had opened a few months before. A refurbished former factory, where you could eat, drink, read a book or a newspaper, or play a game. Best of all, there was a tiny cinema where they showed old films, one after the other, from midnight till dawn.

You could go there at any hour of the night and you'd always find customers. To me, it was like a kind of outpost where you could escape the normal rhythms of everyday life. Day/work/going out/people. Night/home/rest/solitude.

The cinema in particular was fantastic. My ideal kind of cinema.

There were about fifty seats, you were allowed to talk, you could move around, you could drink. Sometimes, between one film and the next, they served spaghetti, or, just before dawn, caffè latte in big cups without handles, and Nutella croissants.

I didn't have to be in court the next morning, which meant I could take things a bit easier. Margherita worked the hours she chose. So we got dressed and went out, both in a good mood.

The place was called Magazzini d'Oltremare. We got there just after eleven, and as usual there were people there, even though it was the middle of the week. Many of those sitting at the tables I knew by sight. Pretty much the kind of people you see in particular venues, at particular concerts or parties. Pretty much like me.

I tried to maintain a stance of ironic detachment from the people who went to these places – more or less on the left, more or less intellectual, more or less comfortably off, more or less over thirty and under fifty (actually, there were also a few over fifty) – but I continued to go there myself. Just like everyone else.

That night the first film on the programme was *House of Games*. One of my ten favourite films. A fantastic story, dark and haunting, about psychiatrists and con men.

There was still at least three quarters of an hour to go before the film started. Margherita saw two women friends of hers at a table, she went up to them and said hello, and they asked us to sit down. Margherita's friends were a couple and were both called Giovanna. They even looked alike. They both dressed in a masculine way, and both moved in a masculine way. It made me wonder who took which role – if indeed there were roles – in the couple. They attended the same martial arts gym as Margherita.

"Are you staying for the film?" Margherita asked.

"No, I don't think so," Giovanna said. "Giovanna has to get up early tomorrow."

"Yes, we're just going to finish this rum and go," Giovanna added.

They were ignoring me a bit. I mean they'd both turned to Margherita, were talking just to her, and I could have sworn the way they looked at her wasn't exactly innocent.

At a certain point, Giovanna asked Margherita if she had decided to enrol with them on the parachute course.

What parachute course?

"I'm thinking about it. I'd really like to. It's something I've been wanting to try for years. But I'm not sure I've got the time."

I managed to cut into the conversation. "Sorry, what's all this about a parachute course?"

"Oh, a friend of Giovanna's teaches parachuting. He keeps asking them to join his course. You can get a licence, you know. They've asked me too."

They've asked you because they want to fuck you. The lesbian licence, that's what they want you to take. That's it – the flying lesbian licence.

I didn't say that. Obviously. We men of the left don't say things like that, though we might think them. Besides, the two Giovannas looked as if they could easily have ripped my balls off and played pinball with them for a lot less.

I kept quiet, while they talked about their parachute course and how great it would be, how it didn't really take up much time – two hours a week, divided between theory and physical preparation – and the fact that you could get a licence after just three jumps.

I felt like making a few acid comments, about how a parachute licence was an essential accessory for a young urban professional woman at the start of the new millennium. And how great it was that you could get that licence after just three jumps. Think of it, guys, *just three jumps.*

I kept quiet, which was just as well. Because having the courage to throw myself out a plane, into the empty sky, without being afraid, was one of my most secret, most forbidden dreams. A dream I'd never had the courage to reveal to anyone, and which I knew perfectly well I'd never have the courage to realize once I'd passed forty.

A dream that lay deep in my childhood fears and

11

fantasies and was still there to remind me that time was passing. And that there were many other things – large and small – that I'd have liked to do and had never found the courage to do. That I *would* never find the courage to do.

They managed to convince her that she could find the time to do the course. They agreed to meet two days later at the premises of the parachute club, where they would all enrol together, with a discount, thanks to the friend of the two Giovannas.

"I'm going to see the film," I said. "It's starting in a few minutes. But don't worry, you can stay and talk." My tone was dignified.

"No, no. I'm coming too. They're leaving."

The two Giovannas nodded. One of them knocked back what was left in her glass, like a real tough guy. They said goodbye to us – well, to Margherita, really – and left.

When we entered the little screening room, the lights were already out and the film was starting. Before abandoning myself to David Mamet's dark, surreal atmosphere, I thought, just for a second, how much I'd like to throw myself into the empty sky, from a plane or somewhere else very high up.

Into the empty sky. Without being afraid.

4

"Do you want to know where I got the money, Avvocato?"

I didn't want to know where Signor Filippo Abbrescia, known as Pupuccio il Nero, had got the money. He was an old client of mine, and his trade was defrauding insurance companies – although whenever he was questioned by the judges he gave his occupation as bricklayer.

The following day, his case – he was accused of criminal conspiracy and fraud – was due to be heard in the court of appeal. He'd come to pay, and I had no desire to know where he'd got the money he was about to give me. He told me all the same.

"Avvocato, I hit the jackpot. On the Bari lottery. First time in my life."

He had a curious expression on his face, Pupuccio il Nero. I told myself he looked like someone who'd spent all his life making money by stealing and now couldn't believe he'd actually won something. I told myself that, like so many others, he'd become a thief and a con man because of a lack of opportunity. I told myself that I was losing my grip and becoming an incorrigible bleeding heart.

So I called Maria Teresa and gave her the money he'd placed on the desk. Then Pupuccio and I talked about what was going to happen the following day.

We had two alternatives, I told him. One was to plead the appeal. At his first trial, he'd been sentenced to four years – not a lot, I thought, for all the cons he'd pulled – and I could try to get him acquitted, but if they decided to uphold the sentence, he'd go straight back inside. The other alternative was to plea bargain with the assistant public prosecutor. Assistant public prosecutors – and even appeal court judges – usually like plea bargaining. Things go nice and quickly, the hearing is over by mid-morning, and everyone goes happily home, or wherever it is they want to go.

To tell the truth, even lawyers like plea bargaining in the appeal court. Things go nice and quickly, and everyone goes happily back to their offices, or wherever it is they want to go. But I didn't say that to Pupuccio.

"And if we plea bargain, how long will I get, Avvocato?"

"Well, I think we can try and get it down to two and a half years. It won't be easy, because the public prosecutor is a tough nut, but we can try."

I was lying. I knew the assistant public prosecutor who'd be in court the next day. He'd plea bargain down to two months if it meant he could get away quickly and not have to do a fucking thing. He wasn't what you'd call a hard worker. But I couldn't say that to Pupuccio il Nero, or people like him.

The way it works, in cases like this, is as follows. I say the public prosecutor is a tough nut. I say I could try plea bargaining but it won't be easy and I can't guarantee anything. I mention a sentence I think I can get with plea bargaining, a sentence that's quite a bit higher than the one I'm sure I'll actually be able to get. Then I plea bargain down to the sentence I've been thinking of from the start, confirm my reputation as a reliable lawyer who's really on the ball, and collect the rest of the fee.

14

"Two and a half years? Is it worth plea bargaining, Avvocato? We might as well go through with the trial."

"Of course we can try," I said in a calm, even tone. "But if they uphold the four-year sentence, you go back inside. As long as you know that."

A professional pause, before I went on.

"Below three years, there's the possibility of probation. Think about it."

His turn to pause.

"All right, Avvocato, but try to get me less than two and a half years. It's not as if I killed anyone. Two or three cons is all I did."

I was pretty sure he'd done at least two hundred, even though the carabinieri had only discovered about fifteen. He was also part of a conspiracy involved in fraud on an industrial scale, and there were plenty of other things on his criminal record. But I didn't see the point of splitting hairs with Signor Filippo Abbrescia.

"All right, Pupuccio. Now you just have to sign the special proxy, and you won't need to attend the hearing tomorrow." That way I'm not forced to play-act in court, I thought, and the public prosecutor and I can get it all out of the way quickly.

"All right, Avvocato, but please, let's try to get the minimum."

"Don't worry, Pupuccio. Come into the office tomorrow, and I'll tell you how things worked out. And when you see my secretary, get the invoice."

He was already on his feet, but was still in front of the desk. "Avvocato?"

"Yes?"

"Avvocato, why bother with an invoice? You'll only have to pay taxes on the money. Is it worth it? I remember when I first started coming to you, you didn't bother with invoices."

15

I sat there, looking him up and down. It was true. For many years most of the money I'd earned had been undeclared. Then, when I'd gone through a lot of changes in my life, I'd started to feel ashamed about that. It wasn't that I'd thought clearly about it. It's just that I was afraid of swindling the tax authorities, and so – nearly always, and according to my own estimate of how much it was right to give to the tax people, in order to do my duty – I started issuing invoices and paid a whole lot of money in taxes. I was one of the four or five richest lawyers in Bari. If you went by my declaration of income.

I couldn't tell Signor Filippo Abbrescia, known as Pupuccio il Nero, these things. He wouldn't have understood. On the contrary, he'd have thought I was a bit crazy and changed lawyers. Which I didn't want. He was a good client, a good man, all things considered, and he always paid on time.

"Customs and Excise, Pupuccio, Customs and Excise. They're all over us lawyers at this time of year. We have to be careful. They hang around outside our offices, and when they see a client coming out, they check if he has an invoice. If he doesn't, they come into the office and start an audit. And I end up out of a job. I prefer not to run the risk."

Pupuccio seemed relieved. I was a bit of a coward, but I was only paying taxes to avoid worse problems. He wouldn't have done the same, but he could understand it.

He gave me a kind of military salute, lifting his hand to an imaginary visor. Bye, Avvocato. Bye, Pupuccio.

Then he turned and went out.

When at least a minute had passed and I was sure he was out of the office, I said out loud, "I'm an idiot. OK, so I'm an idiot. Is there any law against it? No, so I'll be as much of an idiot as I like."

Then I laid my head against the back of my chair and stayed like that, looking up at some vague point on the ceiling.

I don't know how long I stayed like that. Then the phone rang.

5

Maria Teresa answered as usual, after the third ring. After a few moments I heard the buzz of the intercom.

"Who is it?"

"Inspector Tancredi, of the Flying Squad."

"Put him on."

Tancredi was almost a friend. Although we'd never spent any time together outside work, I felt – and I think he felt too – that we had something in common. He was the kind of policeman you'd like to meet if you were the victim of a crime, the kind you'd avoid like the plague if you were the one who had committed the crime. Especially certain kinds of crime. Tancredi dealt with perverts, rapists, paedophiles, that kind of criminal. None of them had been very happy to have Tancredi on their case.

"Carmelo. How are you?"

"Hi, Guido, not too bad. And you?" He had a deep voice, with a slight Sicilian accent. Hearing him on the phone, without knowing him, you'd have imagined a tall, stocky man, with a paunch. Tancredi was only about five and a half feet tall, with rather long hair, always unkempt, and a thick black moustache.

We quickly got through the civilities, and then he said he needed to see me. On a work-related issue, he hastened to add. My work or his? Mine *and* his, in a way. He wanted to come to my office, with someone. He didn't say who this someone was, and I didn't ask him. I told him we could meet after eight, when

I'd be alone in the office. That was fine, and we left it at that.

They arrived about eight-thirty. Everyone had already left, and I went to open the door.

Tancredi was with a woman about thirty, or a bit more. She was nearly six feet tall, had her hair tied in a ponytail, and was wearing discoloured jeans and a worn leather jacket.

A colleague of Tancredi's, I thought, even though I'd never seen her before. The typical masculine style of a policewoman from the street crimes squad or the drugs squad. She must have screwed up and now she needed a lawyer. By the look of her – the look of someone you wouldn't want to mess with – my guess was that she'd beaten up a suspect or someone brought in for questioning. It happens, in carabinieri barracks and police stations.

I showed them into my office, and Tancredi did the introductions.

"Avvocato Guido Guerrieri . . ." I held out my hand, expecting to hear something like "Officer So and So" or "Inspector Whatshername". Tancredi didn't say that.

". . . this is Sister Claudia."

I looked at Tancredi, then looked at the woman again. He had the barest hint of a smile, as if relishing my surprise, but she wasn't smiling. She held out her hand, looking me straight in the eyes, with a strangely fixed expression. It was only then that I noticed the very small wooden crucifix she was wearing around her neck, hanging from a thin leather cord.

"Sister Claudia is the director of Safe Shelter. Have you heard of it?"

I'd never heard of it and he told me what it was.

Sister Claudia still said nothing, and kept her eyes fixed on me. She gave off a very slight scent, but I couldn't have said what it was.

Safe Shelter was a community, housed in a secret location – it was still a secret at the end of the conversation – which provided a refuge for women who'd been victims of sex trafficking, women who'd been rescued from abusive relationships, battered wives, ex-prostitutes, or women who'd turned state's evidence.

Whenever the police or the carabinieri needed to find accommodation for any of these women, they knew the door of Safe Shelter was always open. Even at night or on public holidays.

Tancredi spoke, I nodded, Sister Claudia looked at me. I was starting to feel slightly uncomfortable.

"So how can I be of service?" Even as I was finishing the sentence, I felt like a complete idiot. Like when I find myself saying things like "Hi!" or "How're you doing?" or "Are you all right?"

Tancredi ignored that and came straight to the point.

"There's a woman who works as a volunteer at Sister Claudia's community. Or rather, she used to. Right now she isn't exactly in a fit state to do so. Anyway, let me tell you the story as briefly as I can. A few years ago this woman met someone. She met him after she'd been through a difficult period, though in fact she's never had an easy life. This guy seemed like Prince Charming. Kind, affectionate, loving. Rich. Handsome too, the women say. Practically perfect. Anyway, after a few months, they started living together. Fortunately, they didn't get married."

I'd heard this kind of story before, not just in my work. So when Tancredi paused for a moment, I cut in. "After they started living together he changed. He wasn't as nice to her as he used to be, then he started to turn violent. Just verbally at first, but after a while physically too. To cut a long story short, their life together became hell. Am I right?"

"More or less. As far as the first part of the story goes. Maybe Sister Claudia would like to tell you the rest."

Good idea, I thought. That way she'll stop staring at me like that, which is making me nervous.

Sister Claudia had a soft, feminine, almost hypnotic voice. In complete contrast to the way she looked. I bet she's a good singer, I thought, as she began her story.

"In my opinion, he didn't change after they started living together. He was like that before too. He just stopped acting because he thought he didn't have to any more. From now on, she was his property. He started insulting her, then hitting her, then doing other things she can tell you herself, if she wants to. Then he started hanging around the place where she worked, convinced she had a lover. Trying to catch her. Of course, he never did catch her, because it wasn't true. But that didn't calm him down. It just made him worse. One night, she told him she couldn't stand it any more and if he didn't stop all this nonsense she'd leave him, and he beat her up."

She broke off abruptly. I could tell from her face that she'd have liked to be there when those things had happened. And not just standing and watching.

"The next day, she packed a few of her things, just the things she didn't need any help with, and moved to her mother's. She'd had her own apartment before, but she'd let it go when she went to live with him. And now the harassment started. Outside her office. Outside her mother's place. Morning, noon and night. He followed her. Called her on her mobile phone. Called her at home. At all hours of the day, and especially at night."

21

"What did he say?"

"All sorts of things. Twice, he beat her in the street. One morning she found her car scratched all over with a screwdriver. One evening, she got home to find her bicycle, which was in the entrance hall of the apartment block where her mother lives, all smashed up. Of course, there's no proof it was him. Anyway, to cut a long story short, as you said, Avvocato, her life became hell. The girls in the community and I have been trying to help. Whenever possible we go with her to and from work. For a few weeks she even came and worked in the refuge, which at least is somewhere he doesn't know and can't find her. But that's no solution. She doesn't have a life, she can't go out in the evenings, can't go for a walk, can't go shopping in a supermarket, can't do anything for fear she'll run into him. Or that he'll be following her. So she doesn't go out any more. She stays at home, shut in, as if she's in prison. But he can move around without anyone bothering him."

"Has she reported him?"

It was Tancredi who replied. "Three times. Once to the carabinieri, once to us at police headquarters, and the third time directly to the Public Prosecutor's department. Fortunately, the case was assigned to Prosecutor Mantovani, who's been working on it. She investigated as much as she could, listened to the woman, got hold of the medical reports, and then put in a request for the bastard to be arrested."

"On what charge?"

"Actual bodily harm and threatening behaviour. But it was useless. The judge rejected the request, saying there were no grounds for arrest. This is where things get interesting. Sister Claudia is here to ask you if you're prepared to take on the woman's case and bring a civil action. Two of your colleagues have already refused. A malicious gossip might say for the same reason the judge refused to arrest the man."

I asked him to explain, and he told me a name. I made him repeat it, to make sure I'd understood. When I was certain we were talking about the same person, I let out a kind of whistle, but didn't say anything.

Tancredi told me the rest. As soon as her request for the man to be arrested had been rejected, Assistant Prosecutor Mantovani had asked for him to be committed for trial. When he'd received the summons to appear, he'd gone and waylaid the woman outside her mother's apartment building.

He had told her she could report him as many times as she liked, nothing would happen to him. Because nobody would ever have the courage to touch him. And he'd added that he'd pull her to pieces in court.

That was why she needed a lawyer. Because she was scared but didn't want to turn back now.

Tancredi also told me the names of the two colleagues of mine the woman had turned to before me. One of them had said he was sorry, but on principle he didn't take on civil cases. I knew him well and wondered if he even knew the meaning of the word *principle*.

The second one had said he had too much work on at the moment and so, unfortunately, he couldn't take on the case. Unfortunately, of course.

By now, the woman was desperate and terrified. She didn't know what to do. She had talked to Sister Claudia, and Sister Claudia had talked to Tancredi. To get his advice. He'd mentioned my name and they'd come to see me. Without the woman. They hadn't even told her about this meeting, because if I refused too, Sister Claudia didn't want her to know.

That was the story so far. I shouldn't feel obliged to

take on the case, Tancredi said. If I refused, they'd understand. And they were sure that if I did refuse I wouldn't talk about questions of principle or having too much work.

Silence.

I looked at Sister Claudia. She didn't look like someone who'd *understand*. No way.

I passed my hand over my face, against the grain of my beard, which had grown a bit since morning. Then I pinched my cheek four or five times, between index finger and thumb, still scratching my beard.

In the end I gave a self-satisfied grin and shrugged my shoulders. No problem, I said. I was a lawyer and one client was just like another. As I said it, I knew I was talking bullshit.

It seemed to me that Sister Claudia's features relaxed almost imperceptibly, with something like relief. Tancredi smiled slightly, looking like someone who'd never had any doubt how the game would turn out.

There wasn't much else to say for the moment. The woman had to come to the office in order to sign the forms agreeing to have me represent her. And in order for us to meet, obviously, seeing as I was about to become her lawyer. Then I would go to the Public Prosecutor's department to make copies of the file. I wouldn't have long to study it all. The trial was due to start in three weeks' time. I asked Sister Claudia to leave me a telephone number, and after a moment's hesitation she wrote the number of a mobile phone on a piece of paper.

"It's my number. The telephone's always on."

When they'd gone, I leaned back against the door and looked up at the ceiling. I made the gesture of searching in my pockets for the packet of cigarettes that wasn't there.

6

In normal circumstances I should have gone too. It was already well after office hours. I hadn't been home even for five minutes since I'd left in the morning, and I needed to have a shower and maybe eat something.

But I stayed in the office. I sat down at my secretary's desk. To think, or something like that.

Gianluca Scianatico was a notorious idiot. A typical, well-known representative of the so-called respectable classes of Bari. A bit taller than me, a one-time Fascist thug, a poker player. And a cokehead, so they said.

He was a doctor and worked in a teaching clinic at the general hospital. No one familiar with those circles in Bari thought he'd got where he had – graduating, specializing, passing competitive exams, and so on – on merit.

His father was Ernesto Scianatico, principle judge of one of the criminal sections of the appeal court. One of the most powerful men in the city. Everyone talked about him, his friendships, his extracurricular activities. Always in whispers, in the corridors of the courthouse and elsewhere. Anonymous petitions were said to have circulated, relating to a whole series of matters he was directly or indirectly involved in. It was said that some lawyers and even some magistrates had tried to report him.

Everyone knew that none of these petitions, whether anonymous or signed, had ever resulted in anything.

Judge Scianatico was someone who knew how to watch his back.

For someone in my line of work – a criminal lawyer in Bari – to go up against him was just about the stupidest thing you could do. About half of all cases, after the initial sentence, were referred to his section on appeal. In other words, about half *my* cases were referred to his section on appeal. I was laying myself open to a glorious professional future, I thought.

"Congratulations, Guerrieri," I said out loud, as I'd been doing ever since I was a child, whenever my thoughts clamoured to be heard, "once again you've found a jam to get into. You've crossed the difficult threshold of forty but your tendency to get involved in problems of every size, shape and description is still completely intact. Bravo."

I sat there for a while, getting increasingly anxious, letting my eyes wander over the shelves and the box files that filled them.

Then I got annoyed.

A constant factor in my life is that after a while I always get annoyed about everything.

Good things and bad things.

Almost everything.

Anyway, as my anxiety diminished, I remembered some of the things Tancredi had just told me. About how he'd gone to see her after receiving the summons. What had he said? Oh, yes. That she could report him as many times as she liked, nothing would ever happen to him. Nobody would ever have the courage to touch him. Not him.

So when my anxiety vanished, I started getting angry. It didn't take much to get me to the right point.

"Fuck Scianatico. Father and son. Fuck both of them. We'll see if nothing ever happens to you, you bastard." Out loud again.

Then I told myself it really was time to go home now.

I told myself that mentally. A sign that the din in my brain was fading.

7

Martina Fumai came to my office about seven o'clock the following evening, with Sister Claudia. Maria Teresa showed them in, and I asked them to sit down on the two chairs in front of the desk.

Martina was a very pretty woman with short brown hair. She was wearing quite a bit of make-up, and there was something evasive in her eyes and her manner. She was very thin. Unnaturally thin, as if she'd been on a diet and hadn't stopped when she should. She was wearing a sweet-smelling perfume, and maybe she'd put on more than was necessary.

She spoke in a quiet voice, and as soon as she sat down she asked me if she could smoke. Yes, of course, I said, and she took a thin cigarette out of a white packet with a floral design and lit it. An unfamiliar brand. The type of cigarette I've always hated. She had a cylindrical lighter with the face of Betty Boop on it. That must mean something, I thought.

She thanked me for taking the case. I told her I couldn't see any problems – using those very words, which I usually hate: *I can't see any problems* – and then I asked her to sign the papers agreeing to have me as her attorney.

She asked me if she was doing the right thing, bringing a civil action.

Of course not. It's madness. We'll both be slaughtered. You and especially me. All because when I was a child I read comics featuring Tex Willer and now I'm incapable of turning back when that would be the most intelligent thing to do. Like right now, with this case. As my more pragmatic colleagues have done.

I didn't say that. Instead, I reassured her. I told her not to worry, of course this wasn't a simple case, but we'd do the best we could, we'd be resolute but at the same time tread carefully. And a whole lot of nonsense like that. The next day I would go the Prosecutor's department, talk to the prosecutor and get the papers. Fortunately, I said, the prosecutor, Dottoressa Mantovani, was someone you could trust. That much was true.

I told her we'd meet again a few days before the hearing, after I'd had a look at the papers. I preferred not to talk about the case until I had an idea of what was in the file.

The meeting lasted at least half an hour. Sister Claudia didn't say a word the whole time, just kept looking at me with those inscrutable eyes.

As they left, I threw a glance, almost involuntarily, at her tight jeans. Just for a moment, until I remembered she was a nun, and that wasn't the way to look at a nun.

8

It was the weekend again.

We'd been invited to a party by two friends of
Margherita's, Rita and Nicola. They were nice people,
a bit eccentric, who in order to have more space at
their disposal had moved to a villa just outside the city,
on the old road that runs south between the sea and
the countryside.

Put like that, it sounds romantic. But the villa was
half in ruins, the garden looked like the garden of the
House of Usher, and every night girls from Eastern
Europe congregated a few yards from the gate, in various stages of undress depending on the season. Their
clients' cars stopped practically in front of Rita and
Nicola's house. There was a constant stream of them
until well into the night. Every now and again, the
police or the carabinieri turned up, hauled in the clients and the girls, sent some of the girls back to their
countries, and for a few days the traffic stopped. Then,
within a week, it all started again, just like before.

The countryside behind the villa was populated by
packs of wild dogs and scattered with ruins used as
storage for stolen goods. I could say that with some
certainty, seeing as how one of the fences who used
these ruins was a client of mine who'd once been
arrested while unloading a truck full of stolen hi-fis
into one of them.

None of this seemed to be a problem for Rita and
Nicola. They paid an absurdly low rent for a thousand

square feet, which they'd never have been able to afford in the centre of town. The house was full of the strangest things. And, when there was a party, the strangest people.

Rita was a painter and taught at the Academy of Fine Arts. Nicola had a New Age bookshop, specializing in oriental and esoteric philosophies and practices.

One of the rooms in the villa had mats on the floor and mirrors on the walls. This was where they held seminars on transcendental meditation, tai chi chuan and shiatsu, and study sessions on *The Tibetan Book of the Dead*, Chinese astrology, and so on.

Nicola was a kind of Buddha of Suburbia, like the Hanif Kureishi character. Only he didn't operate in Seventies London, but in Bari in the early twenty-first century. Between Iapigia and Torre a Mare, to be precise.

As I was getting ready to go out, cleaning my teeth in front of the bathroom mirror, I thought I saw something under my eyes. Like a slight shadow, or a slight swelling. I rinsed the brush, put it away, and had a closer look. There were indeed two very slight swellings, between the eyes and the cheekbones.

Bags under my eyes, I thought: those words exactly. Oh, shit.

I stayed at the mirror and, a bit hesitantly, moved the index finger of my right hand closer to one of those . . . things. There it was. I could touch it, as well as see it.

With my finger, I tried pulling down the skin. It didn't seem like mine. It wasn't elastic, but had the slack texture of a slightly worn fabric. At least that's what I thought at that moment.

Then I started to study my face closely in the mirror.

I noticed I had lines at the corners of my mouth, near the eyes, and especially on my forehead. Long, deep lines, like trenches. How long had I had them? How come I had never noticed them before?

I pinched my skin, in different parts of my face, to see how long it took to fall back into place. As I did this experiment, I remembered when I was a child and my great-grandmother used to hold me on her knees and I'd pinch her cheeks. I'd pull them down and then watch as the skin fell back into place. *Very* slowly.

That reminded me of my great-grandmother's neck, all lines and creases. So I checked my own neck. Which of course was the kind of neck you'd expect to see on a forty-year-old man in good health and reasonable physical condition. My great-grandmother, as I didn't stop to think at the time, had been at least eighty-five, if not older.

I was about to start an anxious search for other marks of time – which had obviously passed without my realizing it – when the doorbell rang. I looked at my watch and realized, in this order (a) that Margherita was ready, was knocking at my door, and was probably thinking I was ready too, (b) that I wasn't ready at all, and (c) that maybe I was starting to lose it.

I went and opened the door, didn't mention point (c) to Margherita (and to avoid her noticing it for herself, I also avoided asking her if she thought I had lines or bags under my eyes), finished getting ready in a hurry, and a quarter of an hour later we were in the street. For the rest of the evening, I stopped worrying about time passing and its dermatological ramifications.

You could hear music even before you got inside

the villa. Wind and string instruments, remote, mystical sounds, a few strokes of the gong. The best of Vietnamese New Wave, someone explained to me some time later. The kind of music I love so much I can even listen to it for five minutes at a stretch.

The house was full of incense smoke, and people. Some of them were almost normal.

Margherita disappeared almost immediately into the crowd and the fog. Soon after, I glimpsed her chatting to a tall, thin, bearded guy, about fifty. He was dressed in an impeccable two-button Prince of Wales suit and looked quite surreal in the middle of this gathering. I knew hardly anybody and didn't much feel like talking to the few people I did know. So, almost immediately, I applied myself to the food, which was copiously laid out on a long table.

There was something like a kind of goulash, but it wasn't Hungarian, it was Indonesian, and it was called beef *rendang*. Then there was something that looked like paella, but wasn't Spanish but Indonesian too, called *nasi goreng*. And then there was something that looked like an innocuous Italian mixed salad. It wasn't Italian – it too was Indonesian – and it certainly wasn't innocuous. When I tasted it, I felt as if I'd put an oxy-acetylene torch in my mouth. I don't remember the exact name in Indonesian, but the translation was something like this: green salad with *very* spicy sauce.

But I ate everything, including mango crepes in coconut sauce and a banana and cinnamon dessert. Both of these were Vietnamese, I think, but they were good.

I went for a little walk around the house. I exchanged pointless chatter with various weird people. Every now and again I saw Margherita, still chatting to the bearded guy. I was starting to get a bit pissed off, and I looked around to see if I could cadge a cigarette off someone.

Then I remembered I'd quit, and besides, no one was smoking. Smoking isn't very New Age.

I was sitting on a sofa, drinking my third or maybe fourth glass of organically grown red wine. It tasted a bit like old Folonari, but I wasn't much in the mood for being fussy.

A girl sat down next to me, dressed in Cultural Revolution style. Sky-blue canvas trousers and a jacket/shirt of the same material, with a Korean-type collar.

She was very pretty, a bit plump, nose pierced with a small diamond, long black hair, blue eyes. There was something vaguely dreamy about her, I thought – or vaguely stupid. She started talking without any preamble.

"I don't think much of this Vietnamese music."

So you're not as stupid as you look, I thought. I'm glad. I don't think much of it either, to me it sounds like a serenade for nail and blackboard. I was about to say something like that, when she went on:

"I like Tibetan music a lot. I think it's more suitable for real meditation."

Oh, right. Tibetan music. Perfect.

"Have you ever listened to Tibetan music?"

She wasn't looking at me. She was sitting calmly, almost on the edge of the sofa, looking in front of her. Straight in front of her at some vague spot, like a crazy woman. As I was about to reply, I realized I was assuming the same position.

"Tibetan music? I'm not really sure. Maybe . . ."

"You should. It's the best thing for unblocking the chakras and letting the energy flow. I have the sense, sitting next to you, that you have an intense aura, a great deal of potential energy, but you're not able to let it flow."

I drank a little more of the organic Folonari and

decided to let my potential energy flow. It seemed to me, then and there, that she'd asked for it.

"It's strange. They told me something similar, though not in quite the same words, when I started getting interested in Druid astrology."

She turned to me, and from her eyes it was clear I'd really grabbed her attention. "Druid astrology?"

"Yes, it's a system of astrology based on esoteric principles, developed by the high priests of Stonehenge."

"Oh, yes, Stonehenge. That's that ancient city in Scotland, with those strange stone buildings."

Dummy. Stonehenge wasn't in Scotland, but in England, and as everyone knows, it isn't a city.

I didn't say that. I complimented her on the fact that she'd heard of Stonehenge, we introduced ourselves – her name was Silvia – and then I explained the principles of druid astrology. A discipline invented by me, in her honour, that night. I told her about the astrological rituals performed on the nights of the summer solstice, the astral intersections, the sidereal affinities. Whatever all that might mean.

Silvia was really interested now. It was rare, she said, to find a man so passionate, so knowledgeable, so sensitive.

As she said the word *sensitive*, she gave me a deep, meaningful look. I went to get a fresh supply of organic wine.

"You drink wine?" she said, with a slight touch of disapproval. New Age girls drink carrot juice and nettle tea. By now I was feeling decidedly merry.

"Oh, yes. Red wine is a Druid drink. It's a ritual medium, useful for inducing Dionysian states." I wasn't lying. I was simply saying that wine is useful for getting drunk. Which is what I was doing now. Then it occurred to me to tell her about a remarkable method of divination. Again, of my own invention. It was the reading of the elbow, as practised by the ancient, mystical Chaldean people. As it happened, it was something I knew as much about as I did about the Stonehenge horoscope.

So I explained how, according to ancient Chaldean wisdom, it was possible to read the trajectories of a person's crossed destinies in his or her left elbow. To me, the whole thing was totally meaningless, but she didn't notice.

In fact, she asked me if we could try an elbow reading. I said yes, that was fine. I knocked back the last gulp of wine from the half-empty glass and told her to uncover her left arm.

As I was pinching the skin of her elbow – an essential practice for discovering the trajectories of crossed destinies – I noticed Margherita. Standing in front of the sofa. Right on top of me.

"There you are."

"Yes, here I am. Actually, I've been here for a few minutes. But you were quite busy, if I can put it like that. Aren't you going to introduce your friend?"

I made the introductions, thinking as I did so that suddenly I wasn't having fun any more. Margherita said *Pleased to meet you* – she never says *Pleased to meet you* – with the friendly expression of a hammerhead shark. Silvia said *hi*, with the intense expression of a stone bass.

Then I said maybe it was time to go. Margherita said yes, maybe it was.

So I said goodbye to my new friend Silvia, who seemed rather disoriented.

We said goodbye to a few other people and ten minutes later we were in the car, with the sea racing by on our right and the outlines of the apartment blocks on the sea road a few miles in front of us. To be honest, I have to admit that the sea, the apartment blocks and all the rest weren't in perfect focus, but somehow I managed to hold the wheel.

"Did you have fun with that girl?"

I tried to look at her without taking my eyes off the road. Not an easy task.

"I was just playing a game, you know. I was telling her about Druid astrology."

"And elbow readings."

"Oh, you heard."

"Yes, I heard. And saw."

"Well, I was only passing the time, I wasn't doing anything wrong. Anyway, you didn't seem exactly bored, with that Rasputin in the two-button Prince of Wales suit. Who was he, the secretary of the Philosophers' Association?"

Pause.

"You're great."

"Really?"

"Really. As great as a stiff neck." She paused a moment. "Or better still, toothache."

"Toothache seems more appropriate."

"Yes." She was trying very hard not to laugh. "The things you think of. Reading elbows. You're crazy."

"I think of all sorts of things. Right now, for instance, I'm thinking some things. About you."

"Oh yes? Things that might interest a girl?"

"Yes, yes, I think so."

She paused a moment. I was trying to keep my eyes on the road, which was becoming ever more elusive amid the fumes of organic wine. But I knew exactly the expression Margherita had on her face at that moment.

"All right, then, Druid astrologer, elbow reader, drive on. Let's go home."

9

On Monday morning, I went to the Public Prosecutor's department.

I entered the courthouse through the entrance reserved for magistrates, staff and lawyers. A young carabiniere I'd never seen before asked me for my papers. I said I was a lawyer and he asked again for my papers. Of course I didn't have my pass with me, so the young carabiniere told me to go out and come back in through the public entrance. The one equipped with a metal detector, in case I had a submachine gun under my jacket.

Or an axe. They'd installed metal detectors after a madman had entered the court with an axe stuffed down his trousers. Nobody had checked him, and once inside he'd started to smash things up. When he was finally cornered and disarmed by the carabinieri, he said he'd come to *talk* to the judge who'd found against him in an inheritance case. That must have been his idea of an appeal.

I was just about to turn round and do as the carabiniere had said, when I was spotted by a marshal who was on duty in court every day and knew me. He told the young man I was indeed a lawyer and he could let me pass.

The entrance hall was packed: women, young men, carabinieri, prison warders and lawyers, most of them provincial. It was the first day of the trial of a group of drug dealers from Altamura. The background noise was the kind you hear in a theatre before the show starts. The background smell was the kind you often smell in railway stations, or on crowded buses. Or in the entrance halls of law courts.

I made my way through the crowd, the noise and the smell, reached the lift, and went up to the Public Prosecutor's department .

Assistant Public Prosecutor Alessandra Mantovani's office was in the usual mess. Files heaped up on the desk, on the chairs, on the sofa and even on the floor.

Every time I entered a public prosecutor's office, I thought how glad I was to be a lawyer, not a magistrate.

"Avvocato Guerrieri."

"Prosecutor."

I closed the door, and Alessandra stood up, walked around the desk, avoiding a huge heap of files, and came towards me. We greeted each other with a kiss on the cheek.

Alessandra was my friend, a beautiful woman, and probably the best magistrate in the Prosecutor's department.

She was from Verona, but a few years before had requested a transfer to Bari. She had come on a one-way ticket, leaving behind her a rich husband and an easy life. To come and live with a guy she thought was the love of her life. Even very intelligent women do very stupid things. The guy wasn't the love of her life, just an ordinary man no different from any other. And just like an ordinary man, after a few months he'd simply left her. So she stayed on, alone, in a city she didn't know, without friends, without anywhere else to go. And without complaining.

"Is this a social call or have you started defending perverts?"

Alessandra was in the section of the Public Prosecutor's department dealing with sex crimes. As a rule, I didn't defend that kind of client, and there weren't many civil cases in that section, so Alessandra and I had few opportunities to meet for professional reasons.

"Yes, your colleague next door was picked up in the park wearing a black raincoat, and nothing underneath. He was arrested by a special team from the public hygiene department and he's asked me to defend him."

The colleague next door didn't have what you'd call a spotless reputation. All sorts of amusing stories were told about him. And about the many secretaries, female bailiffs, typists – mostly quite advanced in years – who passed through his office outside working hours.

We joked a while longer and then I told her the reason for my visit.

The first thing she said was that I'd taken on a difficult case. Thanks, but I'd already figured that.

Obviously, I knew who the defendant was, and his father. Obviously, yes, thanks again for the reassuring tone. When I have a problem and need moral support, I know where to come in future.

What kind of case did we have? A disaster, which I already knew. A disaster, from every point of view. Basically her word against his, at least as far as the worst of his actions were concerned. The annoying phone calls were proved by the records, but that was a minor offence. There were a couple of medical reports from the casualty ward, but they didn't show any serious injuries. When the worst offences had been committed, she hadn't sought medical help. She was ashamed to say what had happened. It was always like that. They're beaten up and then they're ashamed to say that their husbands or partners are animals.

"If you want my opinion, I think the Fumai girl was also raped during the period they were living together. It happens a lot, but it almost never comes to trial. They feel ashamed. It's incredible, but they feel ashamed."

"Who's the judge?"

"Caldarola."

"Great."

Judge Cosimo Caldarola was a sad, colourless bureaucrat. I'd known him for more than fifteen years, that is, ever since becoming a trial lawyer, and I'd never seen him smile.

"Give me some good news. Who's our friend's lawyer?"

"Guess."

"Delissanti?"

"Congratulations. You'll see, we won't be bored in this trial."

Delissanti was a bastard. But good, bloody good. A kind of 240-pound pitbull. Nobody was keen to have him as an opponent. I'd seen him cross-examine prosecution witnesses, making them say one thing and then immediately afterwards the exact opposite. Without their even realizing it. For a few seconds I had a disturbing vision of my frail client struggling with Delissanti. It occurred to me we were really in the shit.

I asked if I could see the papers and Alessandra told me they were in the secretariat. I could go along there, take a look at the file, and whatever I needed I could get photocopied.

After all this good news, I stood up to shake off my unease.

"Wait," she said, and started rummaging in her desk drawers. After a while she took out a small wad of photocopies pinned together. She put them in an envelope and held it out to me.

"For copies of the documents, go to the secretariat and pay the fees. These I'm giving you for free. They make for interesting reading, I think. If you want to get an idea what kind of man our friend is."

I took the envelope and put it in my briefcase. We said goodbye and I went off to the secretariat to make copies of the file. Thinking that everything was going really wonderfully.

10

I went to the secretariat, started selecting the documents I might need, and after a while realized I was
wasting time, just to save a bit of money on photocopies and chancery fees. So I told the clerk I wanted a
complete copy of the file and I needed it before the
end of the morning. I paid the fees, with a supplement
to get it done quickly, and that reminded me that I
hadn't even got an advance from Signorina Fumai and
her friend Sister Claudia.

I went back to the office at lunchtime, with a whole
folder full of photocopies.

I told Maria Teresa to order me a couple of rolls
and a beer for lunch from the bar on the ground
floor, and when they arrived I started working and
eating.

There was nothing of particular interest in the file. I
already knew the gist of it.

As Alessandra had said, the evidence against Scianatico consisted basically of my client's statements. There
were some corroborating testimonies, two medical
reports, and the phone records. In a normal trial
that might even have been enough. But this wasn't a
normal trial.

It took me no more than an hour to examine the
whole file. Then I opened my briefcase, took out the
yellow envelope and looked at what it contained.

The photocopies were of a book on criminology by
an American psychiatrist, about a kind of criminal I'd

43

never had to deal with since becoming a lawyer. Or maybe I had, without realizing it. The stalker.

In the first pages, the author, quoting US laws, a large number of studies, and the FBI manual of criminal classification, defined a stalker as

a predator who furtively and obstinately follows a victim according to a specific criterion and acts in such as way as to cause emotional distress and arouse a reasonable fear of being killed or suffering physical abuse, or who in a constant, voluntary and premeditated fashion follows and harasses another person.

In essence, the author wrote, stalking is a form of terrorism directed at a single individual, with the aim of obtaining contact with that individual and dominating him. It is often an invisible crime, until it erupts into violence, or even murder. That's when the police intervene, but by then it's usually too late.

The book went on to explain that many men classified as stalkers hide their own sense of dependency behind a stereotypical, ultra-masculine image, and are chronically oppressive in their dealings with women.

Many stalkers of this kind have suffered traumas in childhood. The death of a parent, sexual, physical or psychological abuse, etc. In other words, stalkers usually have an affective imbalance, reflecting situations in their childhoods that have disturbed their ability to deal with relationships. They are incapable of experiencing the pain of separation in the normal way, of letting go and looking for another relationship. Often their anger at abandonment is a defence against a reawakening of the intolerable pain and humiliation of childhood rejection, which may add to their more recent sense of loss.

It is difficult, the author wrote, to imagine the intensity of the fear and anguish felt by the victim. The terror is so intense and so constant that it is often beyond the understanding of anyone not directly involved.

There was a passage run through with an orange highlighter.

> *As the terrorism escalates, the life of the victim becomes a prison. The victim hurries from the protective cover of home to that of the workplace, then home again, just like a prisoner being transferred from one cell to another. But often not even the workplace is a refuge. Some victims are too terrified to leave home. They live confined and alone, peeking out at the world from behind barred shutters.*

I let out a brief whistle, not much more than an almost soundless breath of air. This was exactly what Sister Claudia had said. *She stays at home, shut in, as if she's in prison.* That's what she'd said, and at the time I hadn't paid too much attention.

Now I realized it was more than just a line.

I picked up the file again and had another look at the charges, which I'd just skimmed through before. The most interesting was that for the offence of threatening behaviour, that is, to all intents and purposes, for stalking. Apart from the abuse, the bodily harm and the telephone harassment, Scianatico was charged:

> *with the offence as under articles 81, 610, 61n.1 and 5 of the penal code, in that with a number of actions carried out with one and the same criminal intention, acting for base and yet senseless motives, and taking such advantage of circumstances of time, place and person as to reduce the possibilities of self-defence, he forced Martina Fumai (after the end of the period during*

which they were cohabitating more uxorio, *in which environment the offence of domestic abuse as described in the preceding charge was noted) using violence and threats, both explicit and implicit, as described in greater detail in the charges which follow: (1) to endure his constant, persistent, persecutory presence in the vicinity of her place of habitation, place of work and places of usual frequentation; (2) to gradually abandon her usual occupations and social relations; (3) to live in her home in a state of substantial deprivation of personal freedom, unable to go out freely without being subjected to harassment, as described above and also in greater detail in the charges which follow; (4) to go to and from her place of work substantially restricted in her personal freedom and with the necessary accompaniment (intended to prevent or resist the attacks of Signor Scianatico) of third parties . . .*

It struck me that this was a kind of situation I'd never really thought about. Obviously there had been times when I'd had to deal with marriages or relationships that had ended badly. Obviously I'd had to deal with the violence and harassment that often followed these endings. I'd always considered them minor deeds. A mere coda to failed relationships. Small acts of violence, insults, repeated harassment.

Minor offences.

I'd never thought about the extent to which these minor offences could devastate the victims' lives.

I went back to the photocopies Alessandra Mantovani had given me.

The stalker is a predator who acts in such a way as to cause emotional distress and arouse a reasonable fear of being killed or suffering physical abuse. It is difficult to imagine the intensity of the fear and anguish felt by the victim. The terror is so intense and so constant that it is often beyond the understanding of anyone not directly involved.

And so on.

I started to feel a healthy sense of anger.

So I closed the file, put aside the photocopies, and started to write out the civil action.

11

Margherita had gone to Milan for two days on business.

So I went straight back to my apartment, with the idea of training for half an hour. Since I'd half moved to Margherita's, I'd created a gym corner in my own apartment, with dumbbells and a punch bag.

Sometimes I managed to go to a real gym, to skip rope, hit the punch bag, fight a few rounds. And get a few punches in the face from younger men who were a lot faster than me these days. At other times, if it was too late, if I didn't have the time or the inclination to get my bag ready and go to the gym, I'd train alone at home.

I was just about to get in my tracksuit when it struck me that it was too late this evening even to train at home. Besides, I was almost satisfied with my work – which didn't happen often – and so I didn't have a sense of guilt, which was what usually got me pounding that punch bag.

So I decided to make dinner. Since being with Margherita, and spending so much time in her apartment, I'd made sure my fridge and my larder were always well stocked. Nor before, but now, always.

I realize it may seem absurd, but that's how it is. Maybe it was my way of reassuring myself that I'd kept my independence. Maybe simply being with Margherita had made me pay more attention to details, in other words, to the things that really mattered.

Whatever the reason, my fridge and larder were full.

In addition, I'd actually learned to cook. Even that, I think, was linked to Margherita. I wouldn't be able to say exactly how, but it was linked to her.

So I took off my jacket and shoes and went into the kitchen to check I had the ingredients for what I had in mind. Cannellini beans, rosemary, a couple of small onions, *botargo*. And spaghetti. That was all.

Before starting, I went to choose some music. I spent a while looking through my collection, then chose Angelo Branduardi's settings of poetry by Yeats. I went back to the kitchen as the music was starting.

I put on water to boil for the pasta and salted it almost immediately. A habit of mine, because if I don't do it straight away I forget and the pasta comes out tasting bland.

I cleaned the small onions, sliced them and put them in the frying pan to cook with some oil and the rosemary. After four or five minutes I added the beans and a pinch of pepper. I left them to fry, and lowered half a pound of spaghetti into the boiling water. I drained it five minutes later, because I like pasta very hard, and tossed it in the frying pan with the seasoning. After putting it on the plate – it spilled over the edge a bit – I sprinkled it abundantly (more than was recommended in the recipe) with the *botargo*.

It was almost midnight by the time I started eating. I drank half a bottle of a fourteen-proof Sicilian white. I'd tried it in a wine shop two months before, and bought two cases of it the following day.

When I'd finished, I took a book from the pile of my latest purchases, still unread, which I kept on the floor next to the sofa.

It was a Penguin edition of *My Family and Other Animals* by Gerald Durrell, brother of the more famous – and much more boring – Laurence Durrell. It was a book I'd read, in Italian, many years before. Well written, intelligent, and above all very funny. Funny as few books are.

I'd recently decided to brush up on my English – when I was younger, I'd spoken it quite well – and so I'd started to buy books by American and English authors in the original language.

I lay down on the sofa and started reading and, almost simultaneously, laughing out loud without restraint.

Without being aware of it, I went straight from laughter to sleep.

A lovely, effortless, serene sleep, full of childlike dreams.

Uninterrupted, until the following morning.

12

When I went to the clerk of the court's office to lodge the civil action, I had the impression the official responsible for receiving documents looked at me in a strange way.

As I left, I wondered if he had noticed which case I was bringing a civil action in, and if that was the reason he'd looked at me that way. I wondered if that particular clerk of the court had connections with Scianatico's father, or with Delissanti. Then I told myself that maybe I was becoming paranoid and let it go.

That afternoon, I had a call at the office from Delissanti. Now at least I knew I wasn't becoming paranoid. The clerk of the court must have called him less than a minute after saying goodbye to me.

Part of Delissanti's professional success was based on his shrewd handling of relations with clerks of the court, assistants, bailiffs. Christmas and Easter presents for everyone. Special presents – sometimes very special, it was said in the corridors – for some people, where necessary.

He didn't waste time beating about the bush.

"I hear you're representing that Fumai girl in a civil action."

"News travels fast. I suppose you have a little bug in the clerk of the court's office."

The clerk of the court was a small, thin man. But Delissanti didn't catch the double meaning. Or if he did catch it, he didn't think it was very witty.

"Obviously you realize who the defendant is."

"Let me see . . . yes, Signor . . . no, Doctor Gianluca Scianatico, born in Bari . . ."

I was annoyed by the phone call, and I wanted to provoke him. I succeeded.

"Guerrieri, let's not be childish. You know he's Judge Scianatico's son."

"Yes. I hope you didn't phone me just to tell me that."

"No. I phoned to tell you you're getting involved in something you don't understand, something that's going to cause a lot of trouble."

Silence at my end of the line. I wanted to see how far he would go.

A few seconds passed, and he regained control. He probably thought it wasn't the right time to say anything too compromising.

"Listen, Guerrieri, I don't want there to be any mis-understandings between us. I'd just like to explain to you the spirit in which I'm phoning you."

All right, I thought. Explain it to me, fatso.

"You know the Fumai girl is unbalanced, psycho-logically speaking, don't you?"

"What do you mean?"

"I mean exactly what I said. She's someone who's been in mental hospitals with serious problems. She's someone who's still in therapy, under psychiatric observation. That's what I mean."

Now he was the one to enjoy a pause, and my silence this time was because I was stunned. When he thought maybe he'd waited long enough, he started speaking again. In the tone of someone who has the situation under control now.

"In other words, we'd like to try to avoid situations we might come to regret. The girl isn't well. She's had serious problems. Young Scianatico was very stupid to take her into his home, but then the relationship finished and the girl made up this whole incredible story. And that other woman, who's a fanatical old-style feminist" – he meant Alessandra Mantovani – "has taken it as gospel truth. Obviously, I've talked to her, but it was no use; knowing her type I should have expected it."

I resisted the impulse to ask him what Martina's psychiatric problems were. I didn't want to give him the satisfaction.

"There's no evidence against my client. Just her word, and you'll soon realize what that's worth in court. This case should never have come to trial. It should have been dismissed by now. So let's avoid making waves, which would only be pointless and damaging. Look, Guerrieri, I'm not saying anything. Check it out yourself, get the information you need, and then tell me if I'm talking rubbish. Then we'll have another word. You'll end up thanking me."

He broke off, but resumed almost immediately, as if he'd just remembered something.

"Oh, and don't worry about your fees. Find a way to get out of the case, and whatever you're owed for the work you've already done, we'll take care of it. You're a good lawyer. More than that, you're a smart fellow. Don't do anything stupid when you don't have to. This is just a petty squabble between a misguided fool and an unbalanced girl. It's not worth it."

Without waiting for my reply, he said goodbye and hung up.

The first time it happened, one summer morning, I was nine.

My mother had gone to work. He had stayed at home with me and my sister, who was three years younger. He was at home because he'd been fired from his job. We were at home because the summer holidays had started, but we had nowhere to go. Except for the yard of the apartment block where we lived.

I remember it as being very hot. But now I'm not so sure it was as hot as all that.

We were in the yard, my sister and I and the other kids. It's odd. I remember we were playing football and I'd just scored a goal.

He appeared on the balcony and called me. He was in beige shorts and a white vest.

He told me to come up, he needed something.

I asked if I could finish playing and he told me to come up for five minutes and then I could go back down. I told the other kids I'd be right back and ran up the two flights of stairs that led to our flat. There were no lifts in those blocks.

I reached the landing and found the door ajar. When I went in, I heard him call me from their bedroom at the end of the corridor. The door of that room was also ajar.

Inside, the bed was unmade. The room stank of cigarettes. He was lying with his legs wide open, and he told me to come closer.

Because he had something to tell me, he said.

I was nine years old.

13

After Delissanti's phone call, I told Maria Teresa I didn't want to be disturbed for the next ten minutes. I always felt a bit stupid telling my secretary *I didn't want to be disturbed, for any reason*, but sometimes it was necessary. I put my feet up on the desk, crossed my hands behind my head, and closed my eyes.

An old method, when I start to feel panicky and don't know what to do.

I opened my eyes again about ten minutes later, looked through my papers, found the sheet with the mobile number, and called Sister Claudia. The phone rang about ten times without any answer and in the end I pressed the red button to end the call.

I wondered what to do next. When I call a mobile phone and there's no answer, I always have the unpleasant sensation that they've done it on purpose. I mean, they've seen the number, realized it's me, and are deliberately not answering. Because they don't want to talk to me. A throwback to my childhood insecurities, I suppose.

My mobile rang. It was Sister Claudia. Clearly, if she was calling me back a few seconds after my call, she hadn't deliberately avoided answering.

"Hello?"

"I had a call from this number. Who is that?"

"Avvocato Guerrieri."

A puzzled silence.

I said I needed to talk to her. Without Martina being

present. It was quite urgent. Could she come to my office, maybe this afternoon?

No, she couldn't come this afternoon, she had to stay at the refuge. None of her assistants was there and she couldn't leave the place unattended. Some of the girls were under house arrest and someone always had to be there, in case the police or carabinieri checked. How about tomorrow morning? Same thing tomorrow morning. But what was the problem? No problem. Or rather, there were a few problems, but I wanted to talk about them in person, not over the phone.

I don't know what made me think of it, but I told her I could come to the refuge myself, tomorrow morning, as I didn't have to be in court.

A long silence followed, and I realized I'd put my foot in it. The location of the refuge was a secret, Tancredi had said. With my spontaneous – and quite unprofessional – suggestion, I'd put Sister Claudia in a difficult position. She could either tell me we couldn't meet at the refuge, because I wasn't allowed there, and even though the fault was mine she'd be forced to say something unpleasant. Or, reluctantly, in order not to offend me, she could tell me to come.

Or she'd give me a good excuse, which was probably the best solution.

"All right, I'll see you here." She said it calmly, like someone who's weighed up the situation and has decided to be more trusting. Then she told me how to get there. It was outside the city, and her directions were so elaborate as to verge on the paranoid.

I set out at ten o'clock the next morning. What with the city traffic and the wrong turnings I took once I was out in the country, the journey lasted nearly an hour. I'd put *The Ghost of Tom Joad* in the CD player when I left. By the time I got there, the disc had finished and I'd just started listening to it again. Before my eyes, the dirt road along which I was slowly advancing became confused with nocturnal images of the American highways, populated by desperadoes.

> *Shelter line stretchin' round the corner*
> *Welcome to the new world order*
> *Families sleepin' in their cars in the Southwest*
> *No hope no job no peace no rest.*

At last, I came to a rusty gate, held closed with a rusty chain and a huge padlock. There was no entry phone, so I gave her a ring on her mobile to come and open up for me. Soon after, I saw her coming round a bend in the avenue, between rows of shabby-looking pines. She opened the gate, and gestured me beyond the bend and the trees, towards where she'd come from, where there was space to park. Then she carefully closed the gate and padlock, while I drove along the avenue of beaten earth, keeping an eye on her in the rear-view mirror.

I had only just parked behind the house – which was actually a farmhouse – and was getting out of the car when I saw Sister Claudia coming back.

We entered the farmhouse. It smelled clean, a mixture of unscented soap and something else, something herbal that I couldn't put a name to. We were in a large room, with a stone fireplace opposite the entrance, a table in the middle, doors on the sides. Sister Claudia opened one of them and made way for me. We went along a corridor, at the end of which there was a kind of square box room, with three doors on each of its sides. Behind one of these doors was Sister Claudia's office. It was a spacious room, with an old desk of light-coloured wood, a computer, a telephone, a fax machine. A bulky old stereo unit, with a turntable. Two small black leather armchairs, both quite old, with cracks everywhere. An acoustic guitar, propped up in a corner. A very slight smell of sandalwood incense.

And there were shelves of books and discs. The shelves were full but tidy. I managed to glance at them just enough to read a few titles in English. *Why They Kill* was one of them. *Patterns of Criminal Homicide* another. I wondered what that was all about, and why a nun would read that kind of book.

No crucifixes on the walls, or at least I didn't see any. Certainly there weren't any behind the desk. There was a poster there, with a sentence printed in joined-up letters, in imitation of a child's handwriting.

Suffer the little children to come unto me, and forbid them not for of such is the Kingdom of God.
                                        Luke 18:16.

In a corner of the poster was a drawing. A child seen from the back, his hands over his head, as if to protect himself against blows from someone you couldn't see. In the foreground, a teddy bear lay abandoned. It was a very sad drawing, and below it something was written. It looked like a kind of logo, but I couldn't read it.

Sister Claudia gestured to me to take a seat in one of the small armchairs and she slid into the other, with a sinuous movement.

In the refuge that morning, apart from her, there were only three girls, two of them under house arrest. They were well hidden, I thought: the place seemed completely deserted.

Well? her eyes were asking.

Obviously. But at that moment I didn't know where to start. It would have been easier in my office. And there was an extra problem: I wasn't sure I really knew why I'd come all the way here.

"There's . . . something more I need to know about Martina. Given that the trial is starting, as you know, in a few days."

"In what sense: *something more?*"

In what sense, indeed? In the sense that Martina may be unbalanced, mad, a compulsive liar, and we're about to get into even more of a mess than we thought at the start?

"I mean . . . as far as you know, has Martina ever had psychiatric problems?"

"What do you mean?" Her tone was much less cooperative now.

"Has she ever been in therapy, ever suffered from depression, ever had a nervous breakdown, that kind of thing?"

Is she *crazy?*

"Why are you asking me these things? What do they have to do with the trial?" The same kind of tone. Or even a bit worse.

All right, you don't want to cooperate. Which means I'm going to make a fool of myself in court, and then when it's all over I'll become the kind of lawyer who deals only with road accidents. If I'm lucky.

I paused for a long time, breathing deeply through my nose. As if to say, I'm being very patient here, but damn it, you have to let me do my job. She said nothing, just waited. She was making me nervous.

"Listen to me, Sister Claudia. Trials are tricky things, they can be quite complicated. That's what lawyers are there for, basically. The fact that a man or woman may be right is almost never enough. In a trial, witnesses are examined and cross-examined, and when a defence attorney cross-examines a prosecution witness, he uses every legitimate means at his disposal to try to discredit that witness. Sometimes illegitimate means too. If we're bringing a civil action, I have to know what Scianatico's lawyer is going to dig up. I have to know if they're going to try and claim that Martina is unbalanced, unreliable, or whatever, so that I can be ready to disprove it."

"I don't follow you. If it can be proved that the man did certain things, isn't that enough? What have Martina's health problems got to do with it?"

"I'm trying to make this as clear as possible, but obviously I'm not succeeding. That's precisely the point: we have to prove that he did certain things. And the only evidence we have is Signorina Fumai's statements. There's not much else to her case. Everything turns on her reliability. Or her unreliability. It's in the interests of a defendant in a case like this, if he has a good lawyer – and in this case he has a *very* good lawyer, and a dangerous one – to spring a surprise and reveal that the presumed victim —"

"*Presumed* victim?"

"Until it's demonstrated in court that someone has committed an offence, that person is presumed innocent. And if he's presumed innocent, then his victim is nothing more than a presumed victim. Whether you like it or not, that's the way it works in this country."

I hadn't raised my voice, but my tone was decidedly tense.

"Martina has had psychiatric problems," Sister Claudia finally said.

"What kind of problems?"

"I don't know if I'm authorized to talk about them. I don't know if Martina wants these things to be known."

60

"They're already known. I mean: Scianatico knows them and his lawyer knows them. He phoned me yesterday afternoon. He more or less threatened me, and told me my client is crazy. I can't not know these things. I could talk to her directly, of course. In fact I'll have to talk to her some time. Even if only to tell her what to expect in court. But when I talk to her, it's better if I know *what* I'm talking about. Do you follow me?"

She leaned her elbow on the armrest of her chair and propped her head on her open hand. She remained in that position for about a minute, without looking at me. Without looking at anything in the room.

"Martina had problems as a child. I'm sure they don't know anything about that. As an adult, she's suffered in the past few years from a form of depression, combined with anorexia nervosa. That must be what they know about."

"When did this happen?"

"Maybe five years ago, maybe more. As far as the anorexia is concerned, the doctors said it was a particularly severe form. She was admitted to hospital and for a few days they had to feed her artificially. With a stomach tube."

"Had she already met Scianatico?"

"No. After she left hospital she was in therapy for a long time. By the time she met that . . . that man, she was cured. Insofar as you can be cured of that kind of problem."

"You mean she had relapses?"

"No. At least not in the sense of being admitted to hospital again. When she's going through a hard time, she has eating difficulties, but that's something she can keep under control. She managed that even at the most difficult moments of her relationship with that man. But there's a doctor following up on her case."

"A psychiatrist?"

"A psychiatrist."

I paused. For personal reasons. A sudden fissure opening on to my past: memories I dismissed, though I couldn't free myself entirely from all the cacophony that went with them.

"And Scianatico knows all about this." It wasn't a question.

"I think he does now."

There wasn't much else to add. I'd feared worse. I mean: Martina wasn't crazy, she wasn't schizophrenic or manic depressive or whatever. She'd suffered from depression and eating disorders, but had recovered. More or less. That was something I could handle in court. Clearly, it wasn't ideal, but I'd feared worse.

"Now all I need is for Martina to tell me about these things herself. Firstly, because I need more details, papers, medical records. The lot. And secondly, because it's the right thing to do. She'll tell me what her problems are – or were – and I'll tell her what we're likely to come up against in court. In the end she's the one who has to decide."

Sister Claudia said all right, she'd come to my office in a few days with Martina. Before that, she'd explain to her what I needed and *why* I needed it.

There followed a few moments of tense silence. Then we both stood up, almost simultaneously. Time to go.

"Can I ask you something?"

She looked me in the eyes for a few moments, then nodded.

"Why did you let me come here?"

After looking at me some more, she shrugged and didn't reply.

We left the farmhouse and walked back the way we'd

come. There was no trace of the girls who lived there. There was nobody. Around us, the wind shook the branches of the olive trees, dislodging the leaves, which were changing colour, brown on one side, a mysterious silvery grey on the other.

We walked slowly until we reached my car.

"Sometimes I'm aggressive. For no reason."

I looked at her without replying, because clearly she hadn't finished.

"It's just that I find it difficult to trust people. Even those who are on the right side. It's a problem of mine."

"I try to get rid of my aggression with my fists." The words just came out, and immediately I'd said them I realized she might take them the wrong way. "I mean I do a bit of boxing. It helps, I think. Like martial arts."

Claudia looked up, slightly surprised. "Strange."

"Why?"

"I teach Chinese boxing."

Well, that was a turn-up for the books.

"Chinese boxing? You mean kung fu?"

"The expression 'kung fu' doesn't mean anything. Or rather it means a lot of things, but doesn't describe any martial art in particular. Roughly translated, kung fu means hard work."

The conversation was slightly surreal. We'd gone from Martina's psychiatric problems to martial arts and Chinese philosophy, with a bit of philology thrown in.

I asked Sister Claudia what kind of Chinese boxing she taught. She told me it was a discipline called wing tsun, which according to legend had been developed in China by a young nun in the sixteenth century. Sister Claudia gave lessons twice a week, in a gym where they did dance and yoga.

I said I'd like to watch one of her lessons. She looked

straight at me for a moment – as if to make sure I was serious and not just making conversation – and said she'd invite me along some time.

We'd reached the end of our conversation. So I made a rather clumsy gesture of farewell with my hand, got in my car and started it, while she went and opened the gate to let me out.

Moving away slowly along the dirt road, I looked in the rear-view mirror. Sister Claudia had not gone inside yet. She was standing next to the gatepost and seemed to be watching as my car drew away.

Or maybe she was watching something else, in some place I didn't know and couldn't even imagine. There was something in the way she stood there, alone, against the background of that solitary, unreal landscape, which gave me a sudden twinge of sadness.

After ten minutes spent in a kind of semi-consciousness, I found myself on an asphalt road, back in the outside world.

14

The following morning I had a trial in Lecce. So I got up early and after a shower and a shave put on one of the serious suits I wore whenever I was working out of town. Wearing a serious suit, usually dark grey, was a habit I'd adopted when I was a very young lawyer. I'd passed my exams at the age of twenty-five, when I still looked like a first-year college student. To look like a real lawyer I had to become older, I thought, and a dark grey suit was perfect for that.

As the years passed, the grey uniform stopped being essential. People knew me in Bari, and besides, as the years passed, I have to admit I looked less and less like a first-year student.

By the time I turned forty, I only put on a grey suit when I went out of town. To make it clear, in places where I wasn't known, that I really was a lawyer. A concept I still secretly had doubts about myself.

Anyway, I put on a grey suit, a blue shirt, a regimental tie, picked up the briefcase I'd brought home from the office the previous evening, left a cup of coffee on Margherita's bedside table, and went out. Margherita was still asleep, breathing peacefully but resolutely.

I'd reached the garage and was just about to get in my car when my mobile rang.

It was my colleague from Lecce, who'd got me involved in that case. He told me that the judge who was dealing with it was ill, which meant that the trial was going to be postponed. So there was no point in my going all the way to Lecce just to hear the order for the postponement. I agreed, there was no point. But how had he found out, at seven-thirty in the morning, that the judge was ill? Oh, he'd known since the day before, but it had been a very heavy day and he'd forgotten to tell me. Bravo. But he would tell me the new date for the trial. Oh, thanks, very kind of you. Bye then. OK, bye. And fuck you.

I don't generally like to get up early in the morning if it isn't absolutely necessary. If I want to see the dawn – it sometimes happens – I'd rather stay up all night and then go to sleep in the morning. Not easy to do, when you've got work the next day. Waking up early – *having* to wake up early – makes me quite nervous.

That morning, I'd woken up early because of my colleague from Lecce. So now I found myself adrift in the city on a lovely November morning. Without anything to do, since I'd supposed the whole day would be devoted to that out-of-town trial which had been adjourned.

Obviously, in a while I'd start to feel anxious and end up in my office going through papers that weren't urgent and making phone calls that weren't necessary. I knew that perfectly well. I know all about anxiety. Sometimes I'm even wise to its tricks and manage to beat it.

Most of the time, it wins and makes me do stupid things, even though I know perfectly well that they are stupid things. Like going to the office on a day when I could go somewhere else and read a book, listen to a record, see a film in one of those cinemas where they have morning shows.

So I would go to my office, but it wasn't eight yet: too early to get sucked back into the vortex of the work ethic. So I thought I'd take a stroll, maybe as far as the sea. I could have breakfast in one of those bars I liked on the seafront.

I could have a nice smoke.

No, not that.

Stupid idea to quit smoking, I thought as I headed towards the Corso Vittorio Emmanuele.

I'd almost reached the ruins of the Teatro Margherita, which was endlessly in the process of restoration, when I saw a vaguely familiar face coming towards me. I screwed up my eyes – I never wore glasses except to go to the cinema or to drive a car – and saw that the man was giving me a kind of smile and raising his arm to greet me.

"Guido!"

"Emilio?"

Emilio Ranieri. We hadn't seen each other for fifteen years. Maybe more. We came level with each other, and after a moment's hesitation he embraced me. After another moment's hesitation I responded to his embrace.

Emilio Ranieri had been my classmate at secondary school, and then we'd been at university together for two or three years. He'd quit before graduating, to become a journalist. He'd started out at a radio station in Tuscany and then was hired by *L'Unità*, where he'd stayed until the paper shut down.

Every now and again I'd hear something about him from mutual friends, though less and less as the years went by. In the mythical period of my life that straddled the end of the Seventies and the beginning of the Eighties, Emilio had been one of my very few real friends. Then he'd vanished, and in a way I'd vanished too.

"Guido. How nice to see you. Damn it, you're just the same, except for a bit less hair."

He wasn't the same. He still had all his hair but it was completely white. There were lines at the corners of his eyes that looked as if they'd been carved in leather: harsh and painful, they seemed to me. Even his smile looked different somehow. There was something scared, defeated, about it.

But it *was* nice to see him. In fact, I was really pleased. My friend Emilio.

"Yes, it is nice to see you. What are you doing in Bari?"

"I work here now."

"What do you mean: you work here?"

"I was unemployed after they closed *L'Unità*. Then I heard they were looking for people here in Bari to join the editorial staff of ANSA, so I applied and they hired me. The way things are these days, I think I was lucky."

"You mean you're back here for good?"

"If they don't throw me out. Not impossible, but I'll try to behave."

While Emilio was talking, I felt a very strange, painful mixture of contentment, anger and melancholy. I'd suddenly realized something I'd been keeping carefully hidden from myself: it was a long time since I'd had a friend.

Maybe that's normal, when you get to your forties. Everyone has their own affairs – family, children, separations, careers, lovers – and friendship is a luxury you can't afford. Maybe real friendship is a luxury after you're twenty.

Or maybe I'm talking bullshit. The fact remains, at that moment I came to the painful realization that I no longer had any friends.

But I was glad Emilio was here with me, glad the trial had been postponed, glad I'd decided to take an hour off.

"Let's go and have a coffee."

"Let's go," he said, again with that scared smile, which looked so incongruous on the face of a man who'd been in charge of crowd control for the Young Communists when they were fighting the fascists on the one hand and the independent trade unions on the other.

We sat down in a little bar on the edge of the old town. I had a cappuccino and a croissant, Emilio just coffee. After drinking it he lit an MS. He'd been smoking MSs since high school. They weren't like Margherita's ultra-slim, ultra-light cigarettes, which were easy to give up. They were a piece of history, a prism for the emotions, a kind of time machine.

When I said no thanks, with a simple gesture of the hand, almost pushing away the packet Emilio had offered me, I noted a kind of disappointment in my friend's face.

Smoking together, I knew well, had always had a special meaning. Like a ritual of friendship.

We talked casually for a while, saying the kind of things you say to re-establish contact when a lot of time has passed, the kind of things you say to find your way again in a terrain that has become unfamiliar.

And so, casually, I asked him about his wife – I'd never met her, all I knew was that Emilio had got married six or seven years earlier, to a colleague in Rome – the usual, commonplace question you ask when you're about forty.

"Are you separated or are you still holding on?"

As I asked the question, I felt a chill descend. Even before Emilio had replied, even before I'd finished saying the words, which were out now and which I couldn't retract.

"Lucia's dead."

The scene turned black and white. Silent and deafening. And suddenly devoid of meaning.

A sentence of Fitzgerald's came into my mind, though I couldn't remember it exactly. In the dark night of the soul, it's always three in the morning.

It got mixed up with fragments of a non-existent conversation in my head, which was running on empty. When did she die? Why? Oh, her name was Lucia. That's nice. It's a lovely name, Lucia. I'm sorry. How old was she? Was she beautiful? How are you, Emilio? My condolences. We have to move on. Why didn't anyone tell me? But who was there to tell me? Who?

Oh shit, shit, shit.

"She got ill and died in three months."

Emilio's voice was calm, almost toneless. As I looked at him in silence, not knowing what to say, he told me his story, and Lucia's. A woman of thirty-four who one day in April went to her doctor to get the results of some tests, and found out her time was almost over. Even though she still had so many things to do. Important things, like having a baby.

"You know, Guido, when something like that happens you think about so many things. And what you think about most is all the time you wasted. You think of the walks you never took, the times you didn't make love, the times you lied. The times you measured out your emotions like so much small change. I know it's corny, but you wish you could go back in time and tell her how much you love her, you think about all the times you didn't tell her and should have. In other words, always. It's not just that you don't want her to die. It's the fact that you wish the time hadn't been wasted like that."

He was speaking in the present tense. Because his time had been wasted.

He told me everything, calmly. As if he wanted to exhaust the subject. He told me how she'd changed, in those few weeks, how her face had grown smaller, her arms thinner, her hands weaker.

I was silent, thinking that I'd never before in my life witnessed grief in such a terrible, clear, pure form.

Such a desperate form.

Then it was time to say goodbye.

We stood up from the table and took a few steps together. Emilio seemed calm. I wasn't. He took out his wallet, rummaged in it for a bit, and took something out. It was a ticket from a coin laundromat, the kind that were starting to spring up in the city, with yellow signs and an American name. He wrote his phone number on it and gave it to me, and I handed him one of my stupid business cards. He told me to call him. In any case, he'd call me.

He seemed calm, but his eyes were somewhere else.

I let it ring three, four, five, six times. With every ring the urgency grew, and the anxiety. I was about to press the button to end the call, and try on the mobile, when from the other end I heard Margherita's voice.

"Yes?"

An offhand tone, the tone of someone who's leaving home to go to work. I was silent for a few moments, because suddenly I didn't know what to say, and I had a lump in my throat.

"Who is that?"

"Me."

"Oh. I was just on my way out, you caught me at the door. What is it? Are you in Lecce?"

"I wanted to tell you . . ."

"What?"

"I wanted to tell you . . ."

"Guido, what is it? Are you all right? Has something happened?" There was a slight note of alarm in her voice now.

"No, no. Nothing's happened. I didn't go to Lecce, the trial's been postponed."

I broke off, but this time she didn't ask anything. She waited in silence.

"Margherita" – as I spoke, I realized I never called her by her name – "you remember that time you sent me a message on my mobile . . ."

She didn't let me finish. "I remember. I wrote that meeting you was one of the most wonderful things that had ever happened to me. It wasn't true. It was *the* most wonderful."

"I wanted to tell you the same thing. Well, not exactly the same . . . but I wanted to tell that I can't explain it to you now . . ." I was stammering.

"Guido, I love you. As I've never loved anyone in my life."

I stopped stammering. "Thank you."

"Thank you? You're a strange guy, Guerrieri."

"It's true. Shall we eat out tonight?"

"Your treat?"

"Yes. Bye."

"Bye. See you tonight."

She hung up. I was standing on the corner of the Corso Vittorio Emmanuele and the Via Sparano. The shops were opening, trucks were unloading goods, people were walking with their heads down.

Thank you, I said again, to myself, and went on my way.

15

The next morning I went straight from home to the courthouse, for a trial. The charge: living off immoral earnings.

My client was a former model and porn film actress, accused of organizing a prostitution ring. She and two other women were the go-betweens for the girls and their clients. She used the telephone and the Internet and took a commission on all completed transactions. She herself serviced a few very select, very wealthy clients. She didn't run a brothel or anything like that. She simply connected supply with demand. The girls worked from home, nobody was exploited, nobody got hurt.

With a commitment surely worthy of a better cause, the Public Prosecutor's department and the police had spent months investigating this dangerous organization. They'd staked out the girls' apartments, and picked up the clients on the way out. More than that, they'd intercepted phone calls and e-mails.

By the end of the investigation, the three organizers were in custody. According to the charge,

> the very clear social danger represented by the three accused, their ability to make confident use, for the purposes of their criminal activities, of the most sophisticated tools of modern technology (mobile phones, Internet, etc.) and their inclination to repeat this antisocial behaviour

makes it essential to impose on them the severest form of custodial sentence, in other words imprisonment.

Nadia had been in prison for two months, then under house arrest for another two months, and then she'd been released. In the early stages of the case, she'd been defended by a colleague of mine, but then she'd come to me, without explaining why she wanted to change lawyers.

She was an elegant, intelligent woman. That morning I had to plead her case using the shortened procedure, in other words, before the judge from the preliminary hearing.

Virtually the only evidence against her came from the telephone and e-mail intercepts. Based on these intercepts it was obvious that Nadia and her two friends had – according to the charges –

organized, coordinated and managed an unspecified but undoubtedly large number of women dedicated to prostitution, acting as intermediaries between the said women and their clients and receiving for such services, and more generally for the logistical support provided to this illicit traffic, a percentage of the prostitutes' income of between ten and twenty per cent . . .

and so on, and so forth.

Reading the papers carefully, I'd realized that there was an error in the procedure for authorizing the intercepts. I was basing my whole case on that procedural error. If the judge upheld me, the intercepts were inadmissible, and there was hardly any evidence against my client. Certainly not enough for a conviction.

When the clerk of the court read out her name and Nadia said she was present, the judge looked at her and was unable to conceal a hint of surprise. With her anthracite-grey tailored suit, her white blouse, her impeccable, sober make-up, the last thing she looked like was a whore. Anyone entering the court and seeing her sitting there, next to me, surrounded by copies of the file, would have thought she was a lawyer. Only much, much prettier than most.

Once the formalities had been dealt with, the judge gave the public prosecutor the floor. He was a scruffy-looking young magistrate, deputizing for the prosecutor who'd carried out the investigations, and he made no attempt to conceal his boredom. I didn't feel very well disposed towards him.

He said that the defendant's guilt emerged clearly from the documents produced at the trial, that a complete reconstruction of the acts committed and the responsibility for them was already contained in the order of application for a custodial sentence, and that the appropriate penalty in such an undoubtedly serious case was three years' imprisonment and a fine of 2500 euros. End of speech.

When Nadia heard that request, she half closed her eyes for a second and shook her head, as if dismissing an annoying thought. The judge gave me the floor.

"Your Honour. We could easily base our defence on merit, examining the results of the investigation point by point and demonstrating that they in no way prove that the defendant has benefited from, or even aided and abetted, another person's prostitution."

That wasn't true. If you examined the results of the investigation point by point it was very clear that Nadia had indeed "organized, coordinated and managed an unspecified but undoubtedly large number of women dedicated to prostitution". Exactly.

But we lawyers have a conditioned reflex. Whatever

the circumstances, our client is innocent, and that's it. We can't help ourselves.

"But the task of a defence counsel," I went on, "is also that of identifying and pointing out to the judge every aspect of the case, which, from the point of view of the investigation, allows him to save time and reach a decision quickly."

And I explained how he could reach a decision quickly and save time. I explained that the intercepts were inadmissible, because there had been no grounds at all for the orders authorizing them. In the case of orders authorizing intercepts, the fact that there are no grounds is an irremediable error. If these intercepts were unusable, I said – and they *were* unusable – it was not even possible to look at them, and there was nothing against my client except a mountain of conjecture, and so on, and so forth. As I spoke, the judge leafed through the file.

When I finished, he retired to his chamber and stayed there almost an hour. Then he came out and read out his acquittal, which included the formula: *The case is without foundation.*

Bravo, Guerrieri, I said to myself as the judge was reading. Then I made a friendly gesture of farewell to him – we lawyers always make friendly gestures of farewell to judges who acquit our clients – and walked out of the courtroom with Nadia.

Her cheeks were flushed, like someone who's been in a very stuffy environment, or someone who's over-excited. She took out a packet of Marlboro Gold, lit one with a Zippo lighter, and took a couple of greedy puffs.

"Thank you," she said.

I nodded, modestly. But I was very pleased.

She told me she would come to my office in the afternoon. To pay. Then she looked me in the eyes for a few seconds, and asked if she could tell me something. Of course, I replied.

"You're a very good lawyer, as far as I can tell. But there's something more. In my line of work, I've learned a lot about men, and I think I can recognize the decent ones. On the very rare occasions when I meet them. I had two other lawyers before you. Both of them asked me – how should I put this? – for a supplement to their fee, right there in the office, with the door locked. I suppose they thought it was normal, after all I'm just a whore, so . . ."

She took a deep drag on her cigarette. I didn't know what to say.

"So nothing. You, on the other hand, apart from getting me acquitted, have treated me with respect. And that's something I won't forget. When I come to the office I'll bring you a book. Apart from the money, obviously."

Then she shook my hand and left.

I decided to go and have a coffee, or whatever. I felt light-headed, like after an exam at university. Or, indeed, after winning a case.

As I was walking along the corridor leading to the bar, I saw Dellisanti ahead of me, in the middle of a group of trainees, young lawyers and secretaries. We hadn't spoken since his phone call to my office.

My first impulse was to turn on my heels, leave the courthouse, and have my coffee in some bar outside. To avoid an encounter. I even slowed down, and had almost come to a halt when I heard these words quite distinctly, in my head: "Are you losing it completely? Are you afraid of that windbag and his band of flunkeys? You'll have your coffee wherever you like and that lot can go fuck themselves." The exact words. It sometimes happens.

So I started walking quickly again, passed Dellisanti and his entourage, pretending not to see them, and walked into the bar.

They joined me at the counter as I was ordering a fresh orange juice.

"Hello, Guerrieri." As friendly as a python.

I turned, as if I'd only just become aware of their presence.

"Oh, hello, Dellisanti."

"Well, now, what have you got to say?"

"How do you mean?"

"Did you check out what I told you? About the girl, I mean."

I didn't know what to say. It was a bother having to say anything at all, and the man knew how to make whoever he was speaking to feel uncomfortable. No doubt about that.

In reality I'd have liked to tell him that he ought to be thinking about defending his client. Accused of serious crimes. And I would think about defending my client. The victim of the same serious crimes.

I'd have liked to tell him not to make any more phone calls like the one a few days ago, that I'd make sure he lost any desire he had to do so.

In other words, the reply of a man.

Instead of which, I babbled something about how things aren't what they seem, and anyway they were different from the way they'd been told to him, and to cut a long story short, I didn't know how to wriggle out of it only a few days after taking the case. Without a valid excuse, I couldn't do anything. Maybe in a few weeks, or a few months, depending on how the trial went, we could talk again.

In other words, the reply of a coward.

"All right, Guerrieri. I've already said what I had to say. Do as you see fit, let everyone take responsibility for his own actions and face the consequences."

He turned and walked out. With all the others, in formation. Perfectly trained.

After a few seconds I shook my head, with the kind of movement dogs make when they're wet and want to shake the water off them, and then went to the cash desk to pay.

"Avvocato Delissanti's already paid," the cashier said.

I was about to reply that I'd pay for my own orange juice, or something like that. Then I thought it best to avoid ridicule.

It's always best, as far as you possibly can.

So I nodded, made a gesture to say goodbye and left.

My good mood after the outcome of that morning's trial had vanished.

16

Martina and Sister Claudia came to the office the day before the hearing.

I didn't get straight to the point. I beat about the bush for a while, as I almost always do. First of all, I told Martina it wasn't necessary for her to be in court the following day. The hearing would consist merely of preliminary issues, the introduction of documents and requests for the admission of evidence. As long as I was there, it was fine.

There was no need for her to miss a day's work, I said.

There was no need for her to get scared before she had to, I thought.

She wouldn't need to be in court until we had to examine her, which would presumably be in a few weeks' time.

She asked me how things would be at that hearing. This was it. We were getting to the point.

I told her how things would be, with all the caution of which I was capable.

First she would be examined by the public prosecutor. Then I would ask her a few questions. Then it would be the turn of the defence.

"This is where things get a bit more . . . complicated. The charges are based mainly on your word, and so the objective of Scianatico's lawyer is very simple: to discredit you. He'll try to do that with every means at his disposal. He'll try to make you contradict yourself. He'll try to provoke you and make you lose your cool.

It's unlikely he'll be gentle, and if he is, it'll only be to make you lower your defences."

I paused, before getting on to the worst part. I looked her in the face. She seemed calm. A bit vague, but calm.

"He'll bring up your health problems, Martina. He'll bring up the fact that you spent time in hospital, the fact that you had psychiatric problems ... I mean psychiatric treatment."

Martina's expression did not change. Maybe she looked just slightly vaguer than before.

Maybe. But almost immediately I felt the smell. Intense and slightly acid.

I've always been sensitive to people's smells, able to recognize them, and to notice when they change.

As a child, whenever I entered a lift I could always tell which of the people in our block had been there before me. And I could even put names to the smells. For example, there was a lady in our block who smelled of bean soup. A sad, pale girl with glasses gave off a smell of old paper and dust. The owner of a delicatessen left a hot, thick smell in the lift, which filled the space and made you feel uncomfortable. Many years later I smelled something similar in a shop in Istanbul. It was so similar that for a moment I thought Signor Curci might suddenly appear, with his thick neck, small head and short, solid arms. A few seconds passed before I was able to escape the olfactory short-circuit and recall that the man had died ten years earlier, while I was still living with my parents. So it was unlikely he'd be hanging around the shops of Istanbul.

Often I notice if a woman is indisposed, from the smell. It's something I don't usually talk about, because it's not the kind of information that puts women at their ease.

I'm capable of smelling and recognizing the smell of fear, which is very nasty, rancid and primeval. I've smelled it so many times in police stations, in carabinieri barracks, in prisons, sitting in on my clients' interrogations. The ones who are most desperate, weakest or simply most scared when they realize they're really in trouble, or just that there's no way out.

The first time it happened was not long after I'd become a prosecutor. I found myself appointed by the court to sit in on the interrogation of a man accused of murder. They called me to the station at night – I was on call – because they had to interrogate him immediately. They said he'd stabbed a bruiser who'd previously beaten him up in a bar. They said he'd been seen by a witness. The little man – narrow, slightly bent shoulders, the bewildered look of a small predator – denied everything. It isn't true, it isn't true, it isn't true, he kept repeating, shaking his head, talking in an almost monotonous voice, quite out of place given the situation. He asked to be confronted with the witness. The witness, he said, was wrong and would surely realize his mistake if he could see him face to face. There was something convincing about the dullness and terseness of his defence, and I started to suspect that the police had made a big mistake. And I think the assistant prosecutor who was interrogating him was starting to get the same idea.

Then came the twist. Two policemen entered the interrogation room. One of them was carrying a small transparent plastic bag, and inside it you could see a big knife, the kind called a Rambo knife, its blade dirty with blood. The two policemen looked like cats who've caught a mouse. The one with the bag dangled it in front of the little man's face.

"Now you're really fucked, arsehole. You should

have found this for us yourself. So what about a confession now, eh? There are more prints on this than in all the files in this station. And they're all yours."

It was obvious he'd have liked to underline his words with a pair of well-aimed slaps. But unfortunately he couldn't – he must have thought – not with a magistrate and a lawyer in the room.

I don't remember what happened next. I know the man stopped denying it and confessed soon after. But I don't remember the exact sequence, what he said, what the public prosecutor asked him, what I said to justify my unnecessary presence. By this point it wasn't important. But what I do remember is the smell, which soon filled that little room in the station. Covering the stench of smoke – the cold stench of years and the warm stench of a night of interrogations – the smell of the people, the paper, the dust, the dregs of coffee in the plastic cups.

It was a sharp, obtrusive, slightly obscene smell. And since that night I've never mistaken it.

Immediately after telling Martina that Scianatico's lawyer would pry into her most personal problems, I smelled that smell. It wasn't very strong, but there was no mistaking it. And it wasn't pleasant. I tried to ignore it as I started giving her instructions on how she should act.

"As we've said, he'll try to provoke you. So the first rule is: don't let yourself be provoked. It's what he wants and we mustn't give it to him."

"How . . . how will he try to provoke me?"

"Tone of voice, insinuations, aggressive questions." Before continuing, I paused for a moment. To breathe, and to glance at Sister Claudia. Her face had the lively expression of a statue on Easter Island.

"References to your problems . . . as I said."

"But what have my problems got to do with the trial?"

Yes, what did they have to do with it? Good question. If you needed a psychiatrist once, does it mean you can't testify? And what about the lawyer? Can the lawyer do *his* job? I asked myself before replying, remembering a few distressing fragments of my own past.

"In theory, and I emphasize, in theory, the fact that a witness has had some . . . behavioural difficulties may be relevant. To assess the admissibility of what he says, to get a better idea of the story behind his statements, and so on. In practice we – I mean both I and the public prosecutor – will be very careful to prevent abuses. But it wouldn't be a good idea for us to object to every question about your health problems . . ."

Behavioural difficulties. Health problems. I stopped to think: I was doing some real verbal acrobatics in order not to call a spade a spade.

". . . your health problems, because then it might look as if we have something to hide. So my idea is this, if you agree. Let's play them at their own game. When it's my turn to question you, I'll be the first to ask you about these things. Your stay in hospital, your therapy, and so on. That way we tackle the subject calmly, we show we have nothing to hide, we take away their big surprise, we prevent them influencing the judge, and we reduce the risk of stress. What do you think?"

Martina turned to look at Sister Claudia, then she looked at me again and nodded mechanically. The smell had become sharper, and I wondered if Sister Claudia smelled it. If she did, you couldn't tell from her face. You couldn't tell anything from her face. I resumed speaking.

"Of course to do this you need to tell me everything calmly."

She lit a cigarette, and looked around as if searching for something on the shelves, the desk or out of the window.

Then she told me everything. A common story, not at all out of the ordinary.

Eating disorders, ever since she was a teenager. Problems with her university studies. Nervous breakdown because of an exam she couldn't pass. Depression, anorexia, a spell in hospital. And then the start of her recovery. Drugs, therapy. Meeting a nurse who also worked as a volunteer at Safe Shelter. Meeting Sister Claudia, the job at the refuge with the girls. Graduation, at last. Work.

The meeting with Scianatico.

And all the rest, which I partly knew already. She also told me a few things I didn't know, about the time she lived with Scianatico and some of his predilections. Very unpleasant things, which we might be able to bring up in the trial, if I could find a way.

She also told me something about her family. A little about her mother. And her younger sister, who was married with one child. But she didn't talk about her father and of course I assumed he was dead, but I didn't ask her.

Martina's story lasted at least three quarters of an hour. She seemed a bit calmer, as if she had at last relieved herself of a burden. She insisted that she hadn't taken any medication for at least four years.

Let's hope she doesn't need to start taking it again after this trial, I thought.

"Can I ask you something?" she said, after lighting another cigarette.

"Of course."

"Will he be in court when I testify?"

"I don't know. He's free to come or not to come. We

won't know until the day. But it shouldn't make any difference to you if he's there or not."

"But will he be able to ask me questions?"

"No. Only his lawyer can ask you questions. And remember: when he examines you, and when you answer, don't look at him. Look at the judge, look straight in front of you, but not at him. Remember you mustn't get into any arguments with him, and that's easier if you avoid looking straight at him. And if you don't understand a question, don't try to answer. Politely, without looking at him, tell the lawyer you haven't understood and ask him to repeat it. And if I or the public prosecutor object to one of his questions, just stop, don't answer, and wait for the judge to rule on the objection. I'll go over all these things the day before your appearance, but try to memorize them now."

I asked if there was anything else they wanted to know. Martina shook her head. Sister Claudia looked at me for a few moments. Then she decided now wasn't the moment for her question, whatever it was, so she shook her head too.

"Everything's fine, then. We'll talk again tomorrow afternoon, and I'll tell you how it went." I said that as I was walking them to the door.

I wasn't at all convinced everything was fine.

When they'd left, I went and opened the windows wide, even though it was cold outside. To get a change of air.

I didn't want the sharp smell of fear to linger in the room too long.

17

I closed the office, returned home, had dinner with Margherita and just as we were going to bed I told her I was going down to my apartment. I had to work, to check some papers for the trial next day, and I'd be up late. I didn't want to disturb her, so it was better if I slept downstairs.

The only true part of this was that I didn't want to disturb her. There are nights when you know you're not going to get any sleep. It's not that there's any particular, striking, unmistakable signal. You just know it. This evening I knew it. I knew I'd go to bed and lie there, wide awake, for an hour or more. Then I'd have to get up, because you can't stay in bed when you can't sleep. I'd have to walk around the apartment, I'd read something in the hope it would make me feel sleepy, I'd turn on the TV, and all the rest of the ritual. I didn't want that to happen at Margherita's. I didn't want her to see me ill, even if it was just from occasional insomnia. I was ashamed.

When I told her I was going to my apartment to work, she looked me in the eyes. "You're going to work now?"

"Yes, I told you. I've got a trial starting tomorrow. There'll be a lot of preliminary issues, it's a tricky case, I really have to go over everything."

"You're one of the worst liars I've ever met."

I didn't say anything for a few seconds. "Really bad, eh?"

"One of the worst."

I felt a tightness in my shoulders, thinking that I used to be quite good at telling lies. With her, though, I hadn't kept in practice.

"What's your problem? If you want to be alone, you just have to say so."

Yes, I just have to say so.

"I don't think I'm going to get any sleep tonight and I don't want to keep you awake too."

"You're not going to sleep. Why?"

"I won't sleep. I don't know why. It sometimes happens. I mean, that I know in advance."

She looked me in the eyes again, but with a different expression now. She was wondering what the problem was, since I hadn't told her and maybe didn't even know. She was wondering if there was something she could do. In the end, she came to the conclusion she couldn't do anything tonight. So she put her hand on my shoulder and gave me a quick kiss.

"All right then, good night, I'll see you tomorrow. And if you feel sleepy, don't stay awake just to be consistent."

I went away with a vague, troubling sense of guilt.

After that, everything went as predicted. An hour spent tossing and turning in bed, in the forlorn hope that I'd been wrong in interpreting the premonitory signs. More than an hour in front of the television, watching a film to the end: *Lure of the Sila*, with Amedeo Nazzari, Silvana Mangano and Vittorio Gassman.

Many interminable minutes reading Adorno's *Minima Moralia*. In the hope, which I tried to keep hidden from myself in order for the trick to work, of boring myself so much that I couldn't fail to fall asleep. I got bored all right, but sleep was as elusive as ever.

By the time I dozed slightly – a kind of laboured

half-sleep – a sickly light and the soft, methodical, remorseless sound of rain was already filtering through the shutters, announcing that it was almost day.

It was still raining as I walked across the city, trying to protect myself with a pocket umbrella I'd bought a few weeks before from a Chinese woman. As usually happens the second time you use an umbrella – and that morning was the second time – it broke, and I got wet. By the time I got to the courthouse, just before nine-thirty, I wasn't in a good mood.

18

The courtroom where Caldarola was due to preside
was in the middle of a very busy corridor. As usual
on trial days, the place was completely chaotic. There
was a real mixture of people: the defendants, their
lawyers, policemen and carabinieri who were due to
testify, a few pensioners who spent their interminable
mornings watching trials instead of playing *briscola* on
park benches. Everyone knew them by now and they
knew and greeted everyone.

A few yards from this group, there were other people
with pieces of paper in their hands, looking lost, or
like people who'd rather they weren't there. They
were right. They were witnesses in the various trials,
usually crime victims, and the pieces of paper told
them they were obliged to appear before a judge and
"in the event of non-appearance not due to a legitimate impediment would be liable to be forced to appear,
accompanied by the police, and would be subject to a
fine of . . ." and so on, and so forth.

Even in the best of cases, they were about to live
through a surreal experience. One that wouldn't
increase their faith in justice.

Between the two groups, the passing crowd moved
in a constant stream. Assistants with trolleys and heaps
of files, defendants looking for their own courtrooms or
their own lawyers, prison warders escorting prisoners
in chains, bewildered black faces, tattooed villains –
obviously regular clients of the courts and police

stations – other villains who you realized after a few moments were police officers from the street crimes squad, young lawyers with unseasonable tans, big collars and big knotted ties, and normal people scattered through the courts for the most varied reasons. Almost never good ones.

All of them would have liked to get out of here as quickly as possible. Me too.

Sister Claudia was sitting on a bench, staring at a grimy wall. In the usual leather jacket, and military-style trousers with big pockets. Nobody had sat down next to her. Nobody was standing too close to her either. For a second or two, the written words *Keep your distance* flashed through my mind.

I don't know how it was that she saw me, because she really did seem to be staring at that wall in front of her and I was coming from the side, through the crowd. The fact is, when I was about six yards away from her, she turned her head as if obeying a silent command and immediately stood up with that sinuous, dangerous, predatory movement of hers.

I stopped in front of her, not much more than a foot away. Encroaching into that bubble where nobody else dared enter. I nodded my head in greeting and she responded in the same way.

"What are you doing here?"

For a fraction of a second, I thought I saw something like embarrassment on her face, even a slight blush. It was only a fraction of a second, and maybe I only imagined it. When she spoke, her voice was the way it had been the other times: grey, like the steel of a knife.

"Martina isn't coming. You told her not to. So I've come to see how it goes and then tell her about it."

I nodded and told her we could go into court. The

hearing would be starting soon, and it was a good idea to be there to hear what time our case would be dealt with. As I said it, I realized I hadn't yet seen Scianatico, or even Delissanti.

19

Sister Claudia sat down behind the rail separating the space intended for the public from that reserved for the lawyers, the defendants, the public prosecutor, the clerk of the court and the judge. In other words, where the trial takes place.

After briefly explaining to her what was about to happen, I went over to the clerk of the court, who was already in his place. In front of him he had two stacks of files: the cases that were due to be dealt with during the hearing.

In theory, at least. In practice, there would be adjournments, annulments, postponements, either at the request of the defence attorneys or else "due to the excessive number of cases in today's hearing". In practice, by the end of the hearing, the judge would only have ruled on three or four of the cases at the most.

Caldarola didn't think it was dignified for a judge to do too much work.

I asked the clerk of the court if I could see the file. I wanted to check the list of prosecution and defence witnesses. I hadn't submitted a list because I took it for granted that Alessandra Mantovani had indicated all the relevant witnesses.

The clerk of the court gave me the file and I went and sat down on one of the lawyers' benches. All still empty, despite the crowd outside.

Alessandra, as predicted, had listed all the requisite

witnesses. Martina, obviously. The police inspector who had been in charge of the investigation. A couple of girls from Safe Shelter. Martina's mother. The doctors. No surprises.

The surprises – unpleasant ones – were in the defence list. There were a dozen witnesses, who would testify:

(1) as to the relations between Professor Scianatico and the plaintiff Martina Fumai during the period of their cohabitation;
(2) in particular, as to what they noticed on occasions during which they frequented the residence of Professor Scianatico and the plaintiff;
(3) to the best of their knowledge, as to the physical and mental problems of the plaintiff and the behavioural implications of such problems;
(4) as to the reasons known to them for the cessation of cohabitation.

But the real problem wasn't those witnesses. They were only there to make an impression. The problem was the last name on the list. Professor Genchi, professor of legal medicine and forensic psychiatry. He was listed as an expert witness who would testify "as to the conditions of mental health of the plaintiff in relation to the witness statements and the documents whose admission will be requested, with the purpose of ascertaining the plaintiff's mental fitness to testify and, in any case, with the purpose of ascertaining the admissibility of said testimony".

I knew the professor: I had seen him in a lot of trials. He was a man you could trust, not like some of his colleagues, who produce accommodating – and well-paid – evaluations of defendants. Claiming that they have serious mental illnesses, that being ill they absolutely cannot remain in prison and must therefore be transferred as soon as possible to house arrest. Needless to say, in ninety-nine cases out of a hundred, these gentlemen are as healthy as can be. Needless to say, these expert witnesses are perfectly well aware of that, but with a nice fee in sight they prefer not to make fine distinctions.

Genchi, though, was someone you could trust, someone judges listened to. Quite rightly. He would never lend himself to coming into court and talking nonsense or giving false testimony. Delissanti had chosen someone who would never let his hand be forced to exaggerate his evaluation. Which meant that he must be feeling very confident.

As I was reading, and getting increasingly worried, I felt a presence behind me. I turned and looked up. Alessandra Mantovani, already wearing her robe. She greeted me in a professional manner – *Good morning, Avvocato* – and I replied in the same way, *Good morning, Dottoressa.*

Then she went and sat down in her place. Her face was a touch tense. Small lines at the corners of her mouth, her eyes partly closed. I was certain she'd already read Delissanti's list.

The assistant who was with her placed two dusty folders on her desk, full of files with discoloured covers. A few minutes passed, and at last Delissanti came in, with his usual retinue of secretaries, assistants and trainees. Almost immediately after, the bell sounded to signal the start of the hearing.

They'd arrived virtually at the same time. The defence attorney and the judge.

It had to be a coincidence.

20

The preliminaries did not take too long.

The judge declared the proceedings open and asked the clerk of the court to read the charges – in full, as required by law. In practice, it isn't usually done. The judge asks the parties, "Shall we take the charges as read?" Then he usually doesn't even listen to the answer, and carries on. He takes it for granted that nobody is interested in hearing the charges read out, because they already know them perfectly well.

That day, Caldarola didn't take the charges as read, and so we had to listen to all of them in the nasal voice of Clerk of the Court Filannino from Barletta, with his strong accent. A thin man, with greyish skin, not much hair, and a sad, unpleasant grimace at the corners of his mouth.

I didn't like that. Caldarola was someone who, more than anything else, liked to get on with things. It was a bad sign that he should waste time on formalities. It must mean something, but I wasn't sure what.

After the charges had been read out, Caldarola asked the public prosecutor to make her requests for the admission of evidence. Alessandra stood up, her robe dropping perfectly along her body as she did so, without her needing to pull it up over her shoulders. Unlike almost everyone else, including me.

She didn't speak for very long. Basically, all she said was that she would prove the offences indicated in the charges by means of the witnesses on her list and the documents that would be shown in evidence. From the way she looked at the judge, I realized she was thinking the same thing as me. That something was going on behind our backs.

Then it was my turn, and I said even less. I referred to the public prosecutor's requests, asked for the defendant to be examined, if he consented, and reserved my observations on the defence's requests until I had heard them.

"Counsel for the defence."

Delissanti stood up.

"Thank you, Your Honour. Here we all are, even though we shouldn't be. The fact is, there are some cases that should never be brought to trial. This is one of them."

First pause. He turned his head to the bench where Alessandra and I were sitting. Trying to provoke us. Alessandra's face was devoid of expression: she was looking into space, somewhere behind the judge's bench.

"A professional man, a reputable academic, a member of one of the most important and respected families in our city, has been dragged through the mud by false accusations based purely on the resentment of an unbalanced woman and —"

I almost leaped to my feet. I had risen to the bait.

"Your Honour, counsel for the defence cannot be allowed to make such offensive comments. Especially at this stage, when he should be limiting himself to requests for the admission of evidence. Please advise Avvocato Delissanti to keep scrupulously to the provisions of the law: to indicate the facts he intends to prove and to ask for the admission of evidence. Without comments."

Caldarola told me there was no need to get excited.

Anyway, it made no difference. The game was out of my hands.

"Avvocato Guerrieri, you mustn't take things amiss. Counsel for the defence needs to explain the context and the reasons for his requests. How else can I tell if these requests are relevant? Please carry on, Avvocato Delissanti. Avvocato Guerrieri, let's try to avoid any further interruptions."

Son of a bitch. I thought it, but would have liked to say it out loud. Bloody great son of a bitch. What have they promised you?

Delissanti continued, at his ease.

"Thank you, Your Honour, you have caught my meaning perfectly, as always. It is indeed obvious that in order to introduce the aspects of the case to which our evidence relates, I must make certain preliminary remarks regarding these aspects. In essence, if we want to make – as in fact we will – a request for an expert psychiatric witness to be heard, then it is important to say, and *to be allowed to say*, that we are doing so because we consider the plaintiff to be suffering from serious mental disturbances, which compromise her credibility and even her ability to testify. Where such things are concerned, especially when the honour, the freedom, the very life of a man like Professor Scianatico are at stake, there is no point in beating about the bush. Whether the public prosecutor and counsel for the plaintiff like it or not."

Another pause. Again he turned his head to our bench. Alessandra was as still as a sphinx. Though if you looked carefully, you could detect a very small, rhythmic contraction of her jaw, just below the cheek-bone. But you really did have to look very carefully.

"And so before anything else we request the admission of evidence demonstrating" – he hissed the words, almost spat them – "that the plaintiff is suffering from psychiatric problems, which will be explained in greater detail by our expert witness, properly indicated on the list, Professor Genchi. A name that requires no introduction. In addition, we ask to be able to prove the continued existence of such problems, the reasons for the separation as verified at the time, and more generally a condition of severe social maladjustment and personal inadequacy on the part of the plaintiff, by means of the witnesses indicated on our list. We also request the examination of Professor Scianatico, who, I inform you as of now, gives his consent to being examined and to answering questions in order to provide further proof of his innocence. We have no comment to make on the public prosecutor's requests for the admission of evidence. Nor those of counsel for the plaintiff, who doesn't, in fact, seem to be making any significant ones. Thank you, Your Honour, I have finished."

As soon as Delissanti stopped talking, Caldarola started to give his ruling.

"The judge, having heard the requests from both parties, and having noted —"

"I'm sorry, Your Honour, I have some observations to make on counsel for the defence's requests for the admission of evidence. If you will allow me."

Alessandra had spoken in a low but sharp voice, in which her slight Veneto accent was just noticeable. Caldarola looked a bit embarrassed, and I thought I also noted a touch of redness on his usually grey face. As if he had been caught doing something vaguely shameful. Which indeed he had.

"Go on, Prosecutor."

"I have no observations on the request to admit the many witnesses indicated on the list. There seem to me to be too many of them, but that is not a matter I intend to raise. At least not for the moment. However, I should like to say something about the request to hear the testimony of Professor Genchi, referred to by counsel for the defence as an expert witness, a psychiatric specialist. I should like to raise a couple of points about this request. One specifically concerns the case with which we are starting to deal today. The other is of a more general nature, regarding the admissibility of such requests. Has Professor Genchi ever visited Signora Martina Fumai? Has the professor ever at least *seen* Signora Martina Fumai? Counsel has not informed us of the fact, even though he has told us with great, emphatic, indeed offensive certainty that Signora Martina Fumai is *unbalanced*. If, as I believe to be the case, Professor Genchi has never visited the plaintiff, I wonder what he could possibly base his expert testimony on. Because counsel for the defence, infringing the essence of the duty of disclosure, has not told us. And this remark brings us to the second point I should like to raise. Is it possible to request a psychiatric evaluation of a witness – or even a defendant – without there being any element in the documents which may allow one to presume that such an evaluation is necessary? I believe this general point needs to be addressed before any decision can be made on counsel's request. Because, Your Honour, to admit such a request without it being based on any factual element of the case creates a dangerous precedent. Every time we don't like a witness, for whatever reason, good or bad, we will be able to ask for a psychiatrist to tell us about his or her most private, most personal problems. And who among us does not have personal problems, depression, addictions? To alcohol, for example. Do these problems not concern only themselves and should they not legitimately remain of concern only to themselves?"

As she uttered these last words, she turned to look at Delissanti sitting there on his bench. Among the various rumours about him, one concerned his inclination for strong alcohol. Even at unconventional times, such as early in the morning, in one or other of the bars near his office. He did not turn. He had a nasty expression on his face, and his jaws were clenched. The atmosphere was turning leaden.

"And so, Your Honour, I strongly object to the testimony of the expert witness named by the defence being admitted. At least until there has been a concrete explanation as to what this testimony relates to, and in what way the things to which it may relate have any bearing on this particular case."

I seconded the public prosecutor's objection. Then Delissanti asked to be allowed to speak again. His tone was not as breezy as before.

"Your Honour, I really can't understand what the public prosecutor and counsel for the plaintiff are afraid of. Or rather, to be honest, I do understand, but I'd like to avoid squabbles. There are two possibilities here. Either Signorina Martina Fumai doesn't have any problems of a psychiatric nature, and so there's no reason to get upset at the prospect of hearing the testimony of a specialist like Professor Genchi. Or else Signorina Fumai *does* have problems of a psychiatric nature. In which case these problems – to refer to them in deliberately reductive terms – should be brought up, so that we may assess how they affect her ability to testify, and more generally, the reliability of her testimony. And in any case, Your Honour, with the aim of avoiding any further squabbles and knee-jerk objections, I am able, as of now, to produce photocopies of the plaintiff's medical and psychiatric records."

Delissanti picked up a sky-blue folder and waved it vaguely in the judge's direction. One of his two trainees leaped to his feet, took the folder and placed it on the judge's bench.

At that point I stood up and asked to be allowed to speak. "Keep it short," Caldarola admonished me: he was starting to get impatient.

"Just a few words, Your Honour." I heard myself speaking and my voice was tense. "First of all, we would like to know how counsel for the defence came into possession of these photocopies. Or rather, we would first like to examine these photocopies, since Avvocato Delissanti has not had the courtesy to place them at the disposal of either the public prosecutor or myself. As should have been dictated by the rules of courtesy, even before the rules of procedure."

Delissanti, who had only just sat down on a chair that barely contained his huge backside, stood up again with surprising agility. His face and neck turned very red. The redness made a strange contrast with the white collar of his shirt, which held his brutal neck like a vice, a neck almost twice the size of mine. He yelled that he would not take lessons in procedure, let alone in courtesy, from anyone. He yelled other things, offensive things I assume, but I didn't hear them because I too raised my voice, and it didn't take long for the hearing to be transformed into what's known as an unholy row.

It sometimes happens. The so-called halls of justice are rarely a place for gentlemanly debates. Not the ones I've been in, anyway. And not Caldarola's courtroom that morning.

The outcome was as bad as it could be. At least for

me. The judge said he was forbidding me to speak. I said I would like parity of treatment with counsel for the defence. He cautioned me not to make offensive insinuations and repeated – "for the last time" – that he was forbidding me to speak. I didn't stop speaking, I didn't calm down, and I didn't lower my voice. I knew I was screwing up. But I couldn't stop. Just like when I was a little child, playing football in the school championship, I'd respond to the stupidest provocations, get into fights, and be regularly sent off.

The outcome was more or less the same as in those football matches. The judge called a five-minute recess. When he came back in, he didn't look very friendly. To keep to the rules, he consented to Alessandra and myself consulting Dellisanti's file. It was a copy of the medical records from a private nursing home in the north, where Martina had spent a few weeks.

Both Alessandra and I again objected to their being admitted and to Genchi's testimony being heard. Caldarola delivered his verbal ruling in his usual monotonous voice, in which there were now hints of malice and threat.

The judge, having heard the requests from both parties regarding admission of evidence;
having noted that all the evidence requested is admissible and relevant to the case;
having noted in particular that the admission as evidence of the plaintiff's medical and psychiatric records and the hearing of testimony from a psychiatric specialist, as requested by counsel for the defence, are both relevant, with the purpose (as expressly allowed in Article 196 of the Code of Criminal Procedure) of evaluating the statements of the said plaintiff and ascertaining her physical and mental fitness to testify in court;

103

having also noted that the behaviour of the plaintiff's attorney Avvocato Guerrieri at today's hearing does not seem exempt from disciplinary censure and must therefore be submitted to assessment by the appropriate authorities;
for these reasons:
all the evidence requested by the parties is admitted;
the beginning of the trial is set for 15 January 2002;
a copy of the record of today's hearing should be sent to the sitting public prosecutor and the Bar Council of Bari so that they may assess, according to their respective expertise, whether there exist grounds for disciplinary action to be taken against Avvocato Guido Guerrieri, member of the Bar Association of Bari.

"You screwed up," Alessandra whispered as we were leaving the courtroom.

"I know."

I searched for something to add, but couldn't find anything. Delissanti was behind us, with his people. They were passing comment, and even though I couldn't make out the words, there was no doubt about the tone. Smug.

I said goodbye to Alessandra and started walking faster, because I didn't want to hear them. Anyone watching the scene, and having seen what had happened before, would have thought I was running away.

Sister Claudia, who had been in court the whole time, suddenly appeared by my side, without my noticing where she had come from.

She walked out with me, without asking me any questions.

104

He didn't hurt me that time. When it was over he told me it was a secret between him and me. I mustn't tell anyone. If I told anyone, bad things would happen.

There was a puppy in the yard. He was a little white mongrel and I'd called him Snoopy. He slept in a box and I used to take him our leftovers to eat, and sometimes a little milk diluted with water. I said he was my dog, even though I knew perfectly well they'd never allow me to take him upstairs to our apartment.

He said if I told anyone our secret, the puppy would die. I went back down to the yard, told the other kids I didn't feel like playing any more, and went and hugged Snoopy. It was only then that I started crying.

Of the times after that one, I don't have such a clear memory. They're all mixed up together. Always in that room, with the unmade bed, the stink of cigarettes. The other smells. The empty beer bottles on the bedside table, or overturned on the floor. The sounds he made as he was . . . finishing. The fear that my little sister, who was often in the next room, would come in and see us.

More than a year had passed – I remember it well because I was in my first year of high school – when he told me I was getting big, and there were things – other things – I ought to know, and that he ought to teach me. It was a rainy afternoon, and my mother was out. She was still working in the afternoons, when she could, because he was still unemployed and we couldn't make ends meet otherwise.

That time he hurt me. He hurt me a lot. And the pain stayed with me for days.

After he'd finished, he told me I was a woman now. As he said it he pinched my cheek, between his index and middle fingers. Like a gesture of tenderness.

At that moment, for the first time, it came into my mind that I wanted him to die.

21

Going to the supermarket relaxes me. It's always been like that, ever since I was a child and my mother and I used to go to the Standa on the Corso Vittorio Emmanuele, go down to the basement, take a trolley, and do the shopping.

I remembered the pleasant sense of cold you felt as you went down the last flight of stairs and walked in between the refrigerated aisles, surrounded by the smell of uncooked meats. The meat in those refrigerated aisles, the vegetables, the cheeses, the plastic: all came together in a single, complex, rather aseptic smell, which for me was the "smell of the Standa". There weren't so many supermarkets at that time, and going to the Standa was a bit like going to the funfair in the Fiera del Levante, which was in September, just before the school term started.

At the Standa supermarket there were some products you couldn't find elsewhere. For example, certain vaguely exotic-looking cheeses in tubs, the names of which I can't remember. The taste, though, I remember well: they tasted of ham, a kind of rustic taste, much more intense than those little triangles I was used to eating, which didn't taste of anything. There were French biscuits that were like little pastries. They were a luxury item, and you couldn't eat them like ordinary biscuits, with milk, for example. And there were so many other things we loaded in the trolley that I always wanted to push it, things that now fill my memory, in the grainy, nostalgic colours of a Super-8 home movie.

I thought then that all kids my age liked going to the supermarket.

I still do. There are afternoons when I can't stand it any more – the clients, the papers, the office, the phone calls to my colleagues – and I feel that I need to get out, to go to a bookshop, or a supermarket. Most of the time it passes, that desire to get out, because there are other clients, other papers, other pain-in-the-arse colleagues to talk to on the phone. Sometimes, though, when I really can't take it any more, I go out. And sometimes I take the car, and drive off for an hour, or even two, to one of those huge hypermarkets on the outskirts of the city.

It gives me a sense of freedom to walk around in the afternoon between the aisles with a trolley and buy the most useless things, the most unlikely foods, books with twenty per cent discount, electronic articles – which I then never use – on special offer. By the time I get back to the office I feel better: not exactly raring to get down to work, but definitely better.

So that afternoon I was in my favourite supermarket. A vast hangar bang in the middle of one of the most rundown areas on the edge of town. An almost unreal place.

I was in the ethnic food aisle, stocking up with Mexican tacos, basmati rice, cans of Thai noodle soup, when, from my jacket pocket, I heard the first rising notes of "Oh Susannah", the latest unlikely ring-tone I'd chosen to personalize my mobile phone. I didn't recognize the number.

"Hello?"

"Guido Guerrieri?" A woman's voice.

"Who is it?"

"Claudia."

I was about to say Claudia who? Then I recognized her.

"Oh, hi," I said, and then immediately remembered we were usually more formal with each other. Why I'd suddenly said hi I don't know. There was a moment's silence.

". . . hi."

I felt embarrassed. I didn't know what to say next. By saying hi, I'd already made things less formal. Sometimes I think I'm socially inadequate: precisely the kind of person who, when they meet someone in the street and they're not sure how to address them, says hi.

"Is everything all right? Is there any news?"

"I phoned your office and they told me you weren't there. Then I remembered you'd called me on my mobile and I'd memorized your number. Am I disturbing you?"

Well, I should be dealing with the delicate matter of the international traffic in spring rolls, but I'll try to fit you in, sister.

Obviously, she wasn't disturbing me.

She told me she was giving a martial arts class the following day. It was open to the public, and if I still wanted to see what it was like, I could come to her gym, which was near the prison. She and her pupils would be there from six to nine in the evening.

I was surprised, but I said I'd be there. She said fine, and hung up. Without saying goodbye.

The following afternoon I left the office at six-thirty, postponing an appointment with a client who was supposed to be coming to pay and so had no objection. I decided to go on foot, even though it was quite far, and by seven-fifteen I was at the address Claudia had given me. It was a gym where they did dance, yoga, that kind of thing. It was called Corpopsyche and as I went in, I was expecting to see something vaguely esoteric, like zen or meditation, full of languid movements and Eastern spirituality. The kind of thing I'm not crazy about.

So I felt suddenly a bit uncomfortable at the idea of wasting time like this that I could have spent working, and I told myself I'd stay just half an hour, out of politeness. Then I'd say goodbye and go back to the office, maybe calling a taxi to get there quicker.

The gym had a parquet floor, a big mirror that occupied one whole wall, and a wall bar for ballet exercises. Exactly what I'd expected, seeing the sign. There were a few benches, on which a dozen people sat watching. I sat down where there was a free space.

If the gym corresponded to what I'd imagined, the things that were happening on the parquet floor – the class itself – were very different. There were some twenty pupils, almost all men. They were wearing black canvas trousers, white T-shirts and black dance shoes. Sister Claudia was dressed in the same way, except that her T-shirt was not white but black. I assumed that distinguished her as a master, like a black belt or something similar.

What they were doing didn't look at all like dance or yoga or some New Age nonsense. They were hitting each other with very quick punches and kicks and blows with the knee and the elbow. Unlike most martial arts, the blows weren't controlled, the movements weren't elegant. It was pretty clear what would happen if these techniques were applied in a real situation, in a street fight for instance.

I was surprised, even though, in a sense, what I was seeing was consistent with the kind of feelings I'd got

110

from Sister Claudia whenever we'd met. As I followed the class, the words for these feelings came into my mind, in this order: direct, rapid, abrupt, aggressive.

Vicious.

The word *vicious*, like the others, materialized spontaneously in my head, by a process of free association. No sooner did I hear it spoken by my inner voice than I felt ill at ease, as if I'd said it out loud. Or as if I'd discovered, and named, something that ought to have remained hidden.

Claudia, the vicious nun.

At a certain point in the session, Sister Claudia took a long black handkerchief out of a bag, placed it over her eyes, and knotted it behind her head. Then she assumed a kind of combat position, while the pupil who seemed to be the most proficient of them placed himself right in front of her. He was a dangerous-looking young man with close-cropped hair, over six feet tall.

At a silent, invisible signal, the student started aiming punches at Claudia's face, and she started parrying them. All with her eyes blindfolded.

I've boxed for many years. I've seen, given, parried, dodged, and above all taken, a lot of blows. In gyms, in amateur rings, even on the street. Before that evening I'd never seen anything like this.

They were moving in a precise, regular rhythm that reminded me of a documentary on the circus I'd seen many years before. TV was still in black and white in those days. There was a rather elderly, pleasant-looking man who was teaching juggling to a group of young people in the ring of an empty circus tent. He too was blindfolded and kept three, or four, or five balls in the air, never dropping them and maintaining the same precise, regular rhythm throughout. It was as if he had magnets on his hands, and the balls were inevitably, irresistibly attracted to them.

Claudia was doing more or less the same thing, but instead of balls there were punches being thrown at her face. She had magnetic hands, and with those magnetic hands she attracted and repelled the punches, rendering them as harmless as balls made out of rags.

In boxing they'd always told us never to close our eyes. In attack and especially in defence. You must never lose control of the situation. *See* what your opponent is doing, catch his move with your eyes as soon as it starts, and be ready to react: to parry, or to dodge and counterattack. I'd always felt comfortable with that idea. Eyes open, always. I associated closed eyes with fear, and open eyes, tritely, with courage. Look straight at the problem, or the opponent, or whatever. One of my few certainties.

At a certain point, the regular rhythm seemed to change. Gradually, the punches, and the parries, gathered speed, and then in a moment it was all over. The pupil was on the ground and Sister Claudia was on top of him, twisting his arm and with her knee on his face. I hadn't really noticed the move that had led to that conclusion.

She took off the blindfold, and all the pupils did relaxation exercises. Then they lined up in front of their master. They bowed slightly in farewell, holding their right fists in the palms of their left hands, their arms flexed in front of their chests.

Only then did she seem to become aware of my presence. She came towards me as the pupils left the floor and headed for the changing rooms.

I stood up, she greeted me with a nod, and I

responded in the same way. I was curious now, there were questions I wanted to ask, and I'd completely forgotten that I'd been planning to get a taxi and go back to the office.

"I've never seen anything like that," I said, not making any particular effort to be original. Opening and parting lines have never been my forte. She didn't reply, because there was nothing to reply.

I tried another tack. "What exactly is the name of this discipline again?"

"It's called wing tsun."

"Not exactly girls' play."

"Most girls' play, like most boys' play, isn't interesting. According to legend, wing tsun was devised by a nun, as a way of allowing physically weak people to defeat bigger and stronger opponents. But there are legends like this in all the martial arts. The best one is about the origins of ju-jitsu. The one about the Japanese doctor and the weeping willow. Do you know it?"

"No. Tell it to me."

"There was a doctor in ancient Japan who had spent many years studying methods of combat. He wanted to discover the secret of victory, but he was disappointed, because in the end, in every system, the thing that won out was either strength, or the quality of weapons, or dirty tricks. In other words, however much you trained and studied martial arts, however strong and prepared you were, you could always find someone else stronger, or better armed, or more cunning, who would defeat you."

She broke off, as if she'd just thought of something that bothered her.

"Does this really interest you, or are you just being kind?"

113

How do you answer a question like that? Especially when asked by a woman – a nun – who's just finished beating up a bruiser over six feet tall as if she were juggling? You don't answer at all. Obviously.

All I did was look her in the eyes with a slightly comical expression, as if to say, *We could dispense with all this point-scoring.* Or else, *I'm not the kind of person who says something just to be kind.*

Incredibly, it worked. Her features relaxed a little, and for the first time her face lost a little of its hardness. It was transformed. Pretty, I couldn't help thinking, and immediately felt ashamed and repressed the thought. Unusual as she was, Claudia was still a nun, and I'd been taught by nuns all through elementary school. Some ideas, associations, patterns of behaviour, are very hard to abandon if you were taught by nuns at elementary school. You just don't say, you don't even think, that a nun is *pretty*.

Claudia resumed her story without making any other comments. I stopped thinking about nuns, both in general and in particular, and my stupid taboos.

"Anyway, this doctor was dispirited, because he wasn't making any progress in his quest. One winter's day, he was sitting by a window. Outside, it had been snowing for hours. He was looking out, deep in thought. The whole landscape had turned white, with all the snow. The meadows, the rocks, the houses, were covered in snow. The trees too. The branches of the trees were heavy with snow, and at a certain point the doctor saw the branch of a cheery tree bend under the weight of the snow and break. Then the same thing happened with a big oak. There'd never been a snowfall like that before."

There's no doubt about it: I have a childish turn of mind. I like being told stories, if the storyteller is good. Claudia was good, and I wanted to know how her story was going to end.

"In the grounds, not far from the window, there was a pond with weeping willows all around it. The snow was falling on the branches of the willows too, but no sooner did it start to accumulate than the branches bent and the snow fell to the ground. The branches of the willows didn't break. When he saw that, the doctor felt a sudden sense of elation and realized he'd reached the end of his quest. The secret of combat was non-resistance. Whoever is yielding overcomes all tests. Whoever is hard, rigid, is sooner or later defeated, and broken. Sooner or later he'll meet someone stronger. Ju-jitsu means: the art of yielding. The secret was in yielding. Wing tsun works on more or less the same lines."

It struck me that if the secret was in yielding, Claudia didn't seem to have mastered it at all. To be honest, she didn't give the impression of being a *yielding* person.

She'd read my thoughts. Or more likely she was simply continuing the speech she had in her head. "Obviously you have to understand what yielding means. It means resisting up to a point, and then knowing exactly when to yield and divert your opponent's strength, which in the end will rebound against him. The secret is in knowing how to find the point of balance between resistance and yielding, yielding and resistance, weakness and strength. That's where the principle of victory lies. To do exactly the opposite of what the opponent expects, which to you comes naturally or spontaneously. Whatever those two words mean."

Yes, I thought. That's true for other things too. To do exactly the opposite of what the opponent expects,

115

which to you comes naturally or spontaneously. Whatever those two words mean.

I remembered a book I'd read a few months earlier. "It's a nice story. It reminds me of what Sun Tzu says in his book on Chinese military strategy."

She looked somewhat surprised. What did I know about Sun Tzu, Chinese military strategy, that kind of thing?

"*The Art of War.*"

"That's the one. He says strategy is the art of paradox."

"Exactly. You've read his book?"

No, I have a manual full of useful quotations for every occasion. I took that one from the chapter entitled "How to Impress Nuns Who Are Martial Arts Masters".

"Yes."

"Why?"

What a strange question. Why? Why do you read a book? How should I know? Because I felt like it. Because I came across it when I had nothing else to read, or to do. Because the cover intrigued me, or the title. Or a few consecutive words on a page opened at random.

Why do you read a book?

"I don't know. I mean, there's no reason. I saw it in a bookshop, I bought it and I read it. The thing that struck me the most was this question of paradox, even though I wasn't sure I understood it when I read it. Now it seems clearer to me."

Claudia looked me straight in the face for a few more moments. She seemed to be changing her mind about the category she'd put me in, whatever that was.

Then she curled her lips, for a fraction of a second. Her idea of a smile. The first. She lifted her hand to say goodbye: a somewhat clumsy gesture, but a friendly one. Then, without saying anything else, she turned and walked towards the changing rooms. Without waiting for my answer.

So I left the gym and looked at my watch. I wasn't going to get a taxi, and I wasn't even going back to the office.

It was almost ten, and it was time to go home.

I set off with my head down. Walking quickly towards the centre of town, past closed shops, past clubs and pubs, with everything I had seen and heard jumbled in my head.

22

Many years ago, in Old Bari, just opposite the moat of Castello Svevo, there used to be a pizzeria. Very small, just one room, with a counter, an oven and a cash desk.

Nino's, it was called. There were no tables – where would they have put them? They made only two kinds of pizza: Margherita, and Romana with anchovies. The pizza maker was a short, thin man about fifty, with a hollow face and feverish eyes that didn't look at anyone. With a baker's shovel, he'd place the hot pizzas on a tiny marble work top, where a fat young man, with a pockmarked, hostile face, would wrap them one by one and hand them over to us with a curt manner. As if he wanted to get rid of us as quickly as possible because he obviously didn't like us. He didn't like anyone.

There were four of us, four friends, and we went and ate the pizzas with our hands, on the low moat wall. The best pizzas in Bari, we would say, burning our tongues and palates, trying to avoid the white-hot mozzarella ending up on our clothes.

I don't know if they really were the best pizzas in Bari. Maybe they were only normal pizzas, nothing different, but we'd feel very Bohemian venturing at night into the old town, which at that time was a dangerous, forbidden place. Maybe they were only normal pizzas, but we were twenty years old and we'd sit on the wall and eat them, and drink Peroni beer from big bottles, and then light our cigarettes. We'd stay there, talking, smoking, drinking beer, until late, endured by the inhabitants of the neighbourhood, until the inhabitants of the neighbourhood went to sleep and the pizzeria closed.

I don't remember what we talked about. The things young men of twenty usually talk about, I suppose. Girls, politics, sport, books we were reading – or that we'd like to write – how we'd change things, how we'd leave a mark, if we didn't burn ourselves out, like so many others had done.

Some nights in late spring, when it was very late, we'd walk back across the old town, which was completely deserted by now and dense with strong smells, dirty, disturbing and beautiful.

The air throbbed with our infinite possibilities, on those spring nights. It throbbed in our eyes that were a little blurred from the beer, in our taut, tanned skins, in our young muscles.

In our raging desire to have it all.

Emilio Ranieri had killed himself on Tuesday. The stupidest day.

That evening, he'd driven out to the perimeter wall of the airport, where many years earlier we used to go at night to watch as the last flight from Rome landed. He'd attached a rubber tube to his car exhaust and put the other end in the passenger compartment. Then he'd closed all the windows, started the engine and waited.

The airport police had found him the following morning. There was no note in the car, or at home. Nothing.

I heard the news in the afternoon, while I was in the office. I carried on working as if nothing had happened, until it was time to close. When I was alone I phoned Margherita.

There was no need to tell her I wasn't coming home that evening.

I went for a walk around the city, in search of memories, in search of a meaning, whatever. Which of course wasn't there.

I walked around the places we'd known. I walked to the seafront, near the monumental entrance to the Fiera del Levante. I walked around the Teatro Petruzzelli, which wasn't a theatre any more, but only an empty red shell in the middle of the city. I sat down on a car opposite where the Jolly, a tiny, legendary third-run cinema, had once been. Now there's only a dirty, closed shutter. I noticed the occasional sad Christmas decoration, blinking intermittently, nervously, on the balconies and in the shops. It was less than two weeks to Christmas.

At a certain point, I even thought of taking my car and driving out to the perimeter wall of the airport.

I didn't do it. Fear of ghosts, maybe. Or maybe just fear that the police would find me, maybe take me to the station and ask me what I was doing there, if I had anything to do with Emilio Ranieri's suicide, that kind of thing. I didn't go because I didn't want to get into trouble. Because I was a coward.

I ended up, late at night, sitting on the wall of the moat in front of the castle, opposite where Nino's pizzeria had been.

It's an area that's never been invaded by the developing nightlife of the last few years. A few hundred yards away there's an invisible border. On the other side, the pubs, the pizzerias, the piano bars, the vegetarian restaurants, the fake traditional taverns, and a constant stream of people all through the night. On this side, around the castle, Old Bari. Just a couple of old beer shops, a woman who roasts meat on an unlicensed stove in the street in summer, another who sells fried slices of polenta. Boys playing football in the street. Previous offenders, being kept under observation, in small groups near the drawbridge. Or rather, what used to be a drawbridge, but is just a small stone bridge now. Police arriving every now and again and taking away those they have under observation, to "take a statement", as they put it. The ones under observation are forbidden to meet among themselves, or generally to meet up with previous offenders. If they do that, they're committing an offence. But they do it all the same. The other previous offenders are their friends. Who else are they supposed to meet and chat to? Their favourite spot is the castle bridge. Everyone knows it, and obviously the police know it too – the police station is a few hundred yards away – and they go there when they need to improve their statistics and make it look as if they're dealing with complaints.

The people involved in the nightlife of Bari don't go near the castle, don't even go anywhere close to it. At this time of night, when the people of the area have gone to sleep, it's deserted there. Just as it was many years ago.

I sat down on the low wall without knowing why I'd come here. Without knowing why I'd been wandering around. Without knowing anything. Looking into space, unable to bring any specific memory into focus. Words, a voice, anything perceived by the senses at any moment of the distant past. In which we had lived before setting out into the dark, unknown future.

"Avvocato, is everything all right? Got a problem?"

I jumped, like when you're just about to fall asleep and somebody shakes you.

It was a dealer I'd defended a few years earlier: I couldn't remember his name. He had a face like a tortoise, good-natured and at the same time absent.

"An old friend of mine killed himself, and I'm feeling sad. Very sad."

He didn't say anything – just nodded slightly – and after thinking about it for a few moments sat down on the wall next to me. We both sat there in silence. The last noises faded away in the alleys of the old town. I felt a strange sense of calm.

After a few minutes Tortoise Face stood up and, still without saying anything, gave me his hand. It seemed natural to me to get to my feet, as a mark of respect.

His hand was small, his grip delicate but not weak.

He walked off in the direction of the cathedral. I set off in the other direction, through the deserted streets, listening to the noise of my steps on the old, shiny stones.

23

After that night, I didn't think any more about Emilio. The days passed, smooth and silent. Without rhythm, without colour. Without anything.

A few days before Christmas, Claudia phoned me. A strange call. She wished me a happy Christmas, I returned the greeting, and then we both fell silent. A silence heavy with embarrassment. I had the impression she'd called me for a specific reason, to tell me something specific, not just to wish me a happy Christmas, and then had changed her mind while the phone was ringing.

The silence continued, and I had the strange sensation of being suspended somewhere, or over something. Then we hung up, and I still hadn't understood.

I don't think she'd understood either.

On 23 December a card arrived at the office, from Senegal. Nothing on it except the words: *For Christmas and the New Year*. No signature.

It was Abdou Thiam, my Senegalese client – a street peddler in Italy, an elementary school teacher in Senegal – who had been tried the year before on a charge of kidnapping and murdering a nine-year-old boy. After being acquitted, he had returned to his country and every now and again sent me cards, with just a few words on them, or sometimes nothing at all. Always without a signature and without his address.

Abdou had narrowly escaped life imprisonment and these cards were his way of letting me know that he hadn't forgotten what I'd done for him. I thought again for a few minutes about that trial and all the things that had happened just before and just after it. It had been less than two years before, but it felt as if a whole lifetime had gone by, and I told myself I had no desire to start thinking about the meaning of time and the nature of memory. So I put the card away in a drawer, with the others, and called Maria Teresa, in order to get through the remaining papers, leave, and let myself be sucked into, and overwhelmed by, the crowded, frantic streets.

We had been invited by some friends of ours for Christmas Eve. Margherita said we should exchange presents before we went out, and so, at nine o'clock, there we were in her apartment, all dressed up, standing next to the little Christmas tree, which was decorated with giant fir cones and thin slices of dried citrus fruit. They were almost transparent and gave off coloured reflections. The apartment was full of nice, clean smells. Pine needles, scented candles, the chocolate and cinnamon dessert that Margherita had made for the party. The cheerful melody of "Bright Side of the Road" was coming from the stereo speakers.

"Empty-handed, Guerrieri? You're running a risk, you know. If you take another book or a CD from inside your jacket, or anything else that isn't a *real* present, I swear I'll leave you tonight and go and get hitched – so to speak – to a South American dance teacher."

"I see I got you all wrong. I thought you were a sensitive girl, not at all materialistic, interested in the arts, literature, music. And besides, I don't see heaps of presents for me under the tree."

"Sit down and wait here," she said, disappearing into the kitchen. She came back a minute later, pushing a huge package, irregular in shape, wrapped in electric blue paper with a red ribbon.

"This is your present, but if I don't see mine you can't even go near it."

"But what about the sheer pleasure of giving, just to make another person happy, with no compensation apart from his gratitude and his smile? What about —"

"No. I'm only interested in barter. Bring me my present."

I shook my head. All right, seeing as how you don't understand the poetry of giving, I'll go.

I went to the door, stepped out on the landing, and came back holding by the handlebars a red, shiny and very beautiful electric bicycle.

"Is this enough of a slap in the face?"

Margherita stroked the bicycle for a long time, as if just seeing it wasn't enough. Like one of those people who get to know things by touching them, not just by looking at them. Then she gave me a kiss and said I could open my present now.

It was a rocking chair, part wood, part wicker. I'd always wanted one, ever since I was little, but I couldn't recall ever telling her. I sat down in it, closed my eyes, and tried rocking.

"Happy Christmas," I said after a minute or two. In a low voice, still with my eyes closed, as if talking to myself in a kind of half sleep.

"Happy Christmas," she replied – also in a low voice – stroking my hair, my face, my eyes with her fingers.

Part Two

24

Left, left, right, another left hook.
Jab, jab, right uppercut, left hook.
Left, right, left.
Right.
The end.

I was lying on the sofa, watching a sports documentary about Cassius Clay/Mohammed Ali. To anyone who has any idea of what really happens in the ring, it's an amazing thing to watch Mohammed Ali's fights.

For example, the way he moves his legs. To understand, you need to have been in the ring. Not many people know this, but the surface of a boxing ring is soft. It isn't easy to skip around on it.

It's an amazing thing to watch the man – a man now afflicted with Parkinson's – dancing like that. A 240-pound man dancing with the lightness of a butterfly. Float like a butterfly, sting like a bee, as he used to say.

Punches hurt, and are usually pretty nasty. Which is why there's something so incredible about that superhuman grace of his. It's as if he's overcome matter, overcome fear, as if he's making a leap out of the dirt and the blood towards a kind of ideal of beauty.

At the end of the documentary, images of the young Cassius Clay – beautiful and invincible – dancing lightly, almost weightlessly, during a training session were intercut with images of the old Mohammed Ali lighting the flame for the Atlanta Olympics. Shaking, concentrating extremely hard to avoid making any mistakes while performing such an easy action, his eyes staring into space.

I thought of how I'd be when I was old. I wondered if I would even notice. It struck me I was really afraid of growing old. I wondered if at seventy – if I reached that age – I'd be capable of reacting if someone attacked me in the street. It's an idiotic thought, I know. But it was what I thought at that moment, and the fear of it went right through me.

So I got up from the sofa as the credits of the documentary were rolling, and took off my shoes, shirt and trousers, leaving just my socks and underpants on. Then I took the boxing gloves that were hanging on the wall, put them on, and set the alarm for three minutes: a regular professional round.

I did eight rounds, with one-minute intervals between them, punching as if a title, or my life, depended on it. Without thinking about anything. Not even my old age, which would come sooner or later.

Then I went and had a shower. My arms hurt and my eyes were a little blurred. But the rest of it was over, for that evening.

25

I met Martina and Claudia in a bar near the courthouse, half an hour before the start of the hearing. To go over my instructions on how Martina should conduct herself.

A few days before, she'd brought me her medical records, and I'd compared them with those Delissanti had produced in court. They were the same. That is, Delissanti's were a copy of ours. As I was comparing them I noticed a detail, which I made a note of in red. It was an important detail.

Martina had memorized well everything I had told her a month earlier. She was nervous, she smoked five or six cigarettes, one after the other, but all in all she seemed to be in control.

When we'd finished going over my instructions, she asked me again if Scianatico would be there that morning. I told her again that I didn't know but that, if I had to make a prediction, I'd say yes. If I were Delissanti, I'd make sure he was in court.

She noticed I'd brought the medical records and asked me what I needed them for. To ask her the questions I'd already talked about, I replied.

I also needed them for something else. Something Delissanti and his client weren't expecting, but I was keeping this to myself. I asked her if she had any other questions. She hadn't, so I said we could go to court.

*

Scianatico was there. He was sitting next to his attorney, looking through the file. He seemed calm. A professional surrounded by other professionals. He was elegant and tanned. Seeing him like that, he didn't look like someone who was having to defend himself against a slanderous allegation. As they say.

I made only a small gesture to greet him and Delissanti, the least I could get away with.

Alessandra Mantovani, on the other hand, wasn't in court. In her place was an honorary assistant prosecutor I'd never seen before. He had very thick eyebrows, hair coming out of his ears and his big nostrils, and rings under his half-closed, slightly bloodshot eyes. He looked like a warthog and had serious problems with even basic Italian.

Holding my breath, I asked him if he had been asked to deputize for the whole hearing. In other words, for our case too. If he had, we could all go home without wasting any more time.

No – Warthog replied – he wasn't deputizing for the whole hearing. There was something Dottoressa Mantovani had to attend to personally and he was to call her when the other cases were over. Then, apparently exhausted by his own eloquence, he collapsed onto the files on the desk in front of him. I noticed he was wearing a wedding ring, and I couldn't help wondering what his wife was like, and if he had conquered her with those beautiful long black hairs coming out of his nose and ears. Maybe she had them too.

Maybe I was going crazy, I thought, dismissing the subject from my mind.

Caldarola arrived, there was a bit of plea bargaining, some summonses were issued, some cases were adjourned. Then the judge retired to his chamber to write out his rulings and the assistant prosecutor/warthog disappeared.

A few minutes later, Alessandra Mantovani arrived. Scianatico and Delissanti stood up to shake her hand, something they hadn't done with me. I didn't like that. Not that I was desperate to shake their hands. But doing that sent a message. It meant: We know that you, Prosecutor, are just doing your job and we don't hold it against you. The real bastard is him – that is, me – and we'll settle our accounts with him when this business is over. Alessandra returned first Delissanti's handshake, then Scianatico's, with an icy smile. Only her lips moved, for a fraction of a second, while her eyes remained frozen, looking directly at them.

That too was a message.

Then the bell rang to announce that the judge was coming back into the courtroom.

We were about to start.

"Right, then, who is the first witness for the prosecution?"

"Your Honour, the public prosecutor wishes to call the plaintiff, Signora Martina Fumai."

The bailiff left the court and his voice could be heard calling Martina's name. A few moments later they came in together. Martina was in jeans, a high-necked sweater and a jacket.

She sat down, gave her personal details, and then the clerk of the court passed her the plastic-coated card, dirty with the thousand hands that had touched it, containing the words witnesses had to recite before giving evidence.

"Conscious of the moral and legal responsibility I assume with my testimony, I swear to tell the whole truth and not to conceal anything of which I have knowledge."

Martina's voice was thin, but quite firm. She was looking in front of her and seemed to be concentrating hard.

"The public prosecutor may proceed with the examination."

"Good morning, Dottoressa Fumai. Could you tell us when you met the defendant, Gianluca Scianatico?"

Alessandra Mantovani was born to do this work. She questioned Martina for more than an hour, without making any mistakes. Her questions were brief, clear, simple. The tone was professional, but not cold. Martina told her story in detail and there wasn't a single objection in the whole of the examination. By the time my turn came, there was, as I'd expected, very little left to ask. To all intents and purposes, just the issue of her stay in hospital and her psychiatric problems. The judge gave me the floor, and from his tone it was very clear he hadn't forgotten what had happened at the previous hearing.

"Dottoressa Fumai, you've given very detailed answers to the public prosecutor's questions. I shan't go back over the same points. I just need to ask you a few questions about some matters relating to your past. Is that all right?"

"Yes."

"In the past, have you had any problems of a nervous nature?"

"Yes. I had a nervous breakdown."

"Could you tell us if that was before or after you met the defendant?"

"It was before."

"Could you please tell us when, and also tell us briefly the cause of this breakdown."

"I think two . . . maybe three years before we met. I was having problems connected with my studies."

"Could you briefly explain to us the nature of these problems?"

"I was finding it impossible to graduate. I had just one exam left, I'd taken it several times without passing . . . and to cut a long story short, at a certain point I had a breakdown."

"I realize how painful it must be for you to recall these events, but could you tell us what happened?"

On my right, Delissanti and Scianatico were talking excitedly. They hadn't been expecting this. I could imagine the insinuating questions they must have prepared. Have you had any psychiatric *illnesses*? Were you treated with psychotropic drugs? Are you mad? And so on. They'd put all their eggs in one basket and now, I thought, smugly, I'd broken them. Fuck them.

"After taking the exam five times, I was desperate. I'd had a very difficult time at university. With only one exam left, I thought I'd got through it. Instead of which, I couldn't get past the final hurdle. For my sixth attempt I studied like mad, fourteen hours a day, maybe even more. I couldn't sleep and was forced to take tranquillizers. The night before the exam I stayed awake, trying to revise. The next morning, when my turn came, I'd fallen asleep on the bench and didn't hear them call me."

"How old were you then? And how old are you now?"

"I was twenty-eight, twenty-nine. I'm thirty-five now."

"And that was when you consulted a specialist?"

"After about ten days, I was admitted to hospital."

"Could you tell us what your symptoms were?"

She paused. This was the most difficult moment. If we could get through this, the rest would be easy.

135

Martina breathed in, and her breathing was laboured, halting, as if there were a valve stopping her from taking a deep breath.

"I wasn't interested in anything, I thought about death, I cried a lot. I'd wake up early in the morning, when it was still dark, feeling panicky. Physically I felt very weak, I had constant headaches, and pains all over my body. Most of all, I had severe eating difficulties. I couldn't feed myself. Every time I tried to swallow something, I'd throw up straight away."

She paused again, as if gathering her strength.

"They had to feed me artificially. With a drip and also a stomach tube."

I let the harshness of the story sink in, before continuing with my other questions.

"Did you have any disorders of perception, hallucinations, that kind of thing?"

For the first time, Martina looked away from the vague point in front of her, on which she had been concentrating, in accordance with my instructions, since the beginning of her testimony. She turned to look at me. In surprise. What did I mean? What did hallucinations have to do with anything?

"Did you have hallucinations, Dottoressa Fumai? Did you see things that didn't exist, did you hear voices?"

"No, of course not. I wasn't . . . I'm not mad. I had a nervous breakdown."

"How long did you stay in hospital?"

"Three weeks, maybe a little more."

"Why did they discharge you?"

"Because I'd started to feed myself again."

"And after that?"

"I had sessions with a therapist, and I took medication."

"How long did the treatment last?"

"The medication, a few months. The psychotherapy sessions . . . maybe a year and a half."

"And you finally graduated?"

"Yes."

"Had you already graduated when you met the defendant?"

"Yes, I was already working."

"Were you still in therapy when you met the defendant?"

"No, the therapy itself had finished. But every three or four months I had a meeting with my therapist. They were like . . . I suppose you could call them check-ups."

"During your relationship with the defendant, did you tell him about the problems you've just told us about?"

"Of course."

"Do you have a copy of the medical records from the time you spent in hospital?"

"Yes."

"Did you have it during the time you lived with the defendant?"

Another pause. Another puzzled look. Martina didn't know where I was trying to go with this. But I knew. And so, probably, did Delissanti and Scianatico.

"Of course."

"Are these the medical records? Your Honour, may I approach the witness and show her these documents?"

Caldarola nodded and made a gesture with his hand. I could approach. Thank you, arsehole.

Martina looked at the papers for a few moments. It didn't take her long to recognize them, seeing as how she was the one who'd given them to me. She looked up at me. Yes, these were her medical records. Yes, the ones she'd had at home when she lived with Scianatico. No, she'd never taken any particular care of them. She hadn't put them in a safe, or even locked them in a drawer.

"Thank you, Dottoressa Fumai. I have no more questions for the moment, Your Honour. But I request that the documents shown to the witness and identified by her be admitted to the case file."

Dellisanti fell for it and objected. I should have requested this admission at the preliminary hearing, he said, without even standing up. Besides, as far as he could tell, these were the same records which the defence had already produced. The request was therefore superfluous.

"Your Honour, I might say that if these are the same documents already produced by counsel for the defence, I don't see why there should be any objection. Or perhaps I do see, but we shall look at that at the appropriate moment. Yes, it is true, these are the same documents produced by counsel for the defence. Theirs are a copy and so are ours, taken directly from the medical records of the nursing home. But on our copy there are a few annotations in pen, made by the doctor who treated the plaintiff after her admission to hospital. As I said, the annotations on our copy are in pen. So we could say that our documents are both a copy and an original. One only has to look at our documents and those produced by the defence to realize that theirs are a copy of ours. For reasons that we will explain further in the course of the hearing, but which you, Your Honour, have surely already realized, the admission of our copy is relevant."

Caldarola couldn't find any arguments to refuse my request, and those put forward by Delissanti were really insubstantial. So he allowed the admission of the documents and then ordered a ten-minute recess before cross-examination.

26

When Caldarola told Delissanti that he could proceed with the cross-examination, Delissanti replied, without even lifting his head, "Thank you, Your Honour, just a moment." He was rummaging among his papers, as if searching for a document without which he couldn't start his questioning.

He was faking it. It was a trick, to make Martina feel tenser, to force her to turn to him and meet his eyes. But she was good. She didn't move a muscle, didn't turn towards the defence bench, and in the end, when the silence was starting to be embarrassing, it was Delissanti who gave in. He closed his file, without taking anything out, and began.

You lost the first round, fatso, I thought.

"If I understand correctly, you have regular meetings with a psychiatrist. Is that right, Signorina?" The way he said *Signorina*, it was clear he meant it as an insult. In other words: a woman who's pushing middle age and hasn't yet found a husband.

"We meet every three or four months. It's a kind of counselling session. And he's a psychotherapist."

"Am I correct in saying that since your nervous breakdown and your admission to a psychiatric ward, you have never stopped treatment for your mental disorder?"

I half rose, with my hands on the desk.

"Objection, Your Honour. Put in those terms the question is inadmissible. Its purpose is not to get an answer, not to elicit information from the witness which may help in reaching a decision, but only to obtain an offensive and intimidating effect."

"Don't judge counsel's intentions, Avvocato Guerrieri. Let us hear what the witness has to say. Answer the question, Signorina. Is it true you have never stopped therapy?"

"No, Your Honour, it isn't true. The therapy itself lasted, as I've said before, a year and a half, maybe a little more. During that time, I had two sessions a week with my therapist. Then we reduced it to once a week, then twice a month . . ."

"Let me rephrase the question, Signorina. Is it correct to say that you have *never* stopped seeing the psychiatrist, but you simply see him less frequently?"

"If you put it like that —"

"Can you tell me if you have ever stopped seeing the psychiatrist? Yes or no?"

Martina clenched her mouth shut and her lips became very thin. For a moment, I had the absurd feeling that she was going to get up and walk out without saying another word.

"I've never stopped seeing the psychotherapist. I see him three or four times a year."

"When was the last time you paid a visit to your psychiatrist?"

He kept repeating the word *psychiatrist*. It suggested a stronger, even if implicit, connection with the idea of mental illness. It was a simple trick, and a dirty one, but it made sense from his point of view.

"They aren't visits, we just meet and talk."

"You haven't answered my question."

"The last time I went to my . . ."

"Yes."

". . . a week ago."

"Ah, how fortuitous. Since you insist on calling this person a psychotherapist, and just so that we can clear up any ambiguity: is he a doctor specializing in psychiatry or a psychologist?"

"He's a doctor."

"Specializing in psychiatry?"

"Yes."

"Why do you still see him if, as you say, you're cured?"

"He considers it advisable for us to meet and check how things are in general —"

"Excuse me for interrupting, but I find this interesting. It's the psychiatrist himself who considers these occasional meetings necessary?"

"It's not that he considers them necessary —"

"Excuse me. Did your psychiatrist say to you at a certain point, when he considered that your mental condition had improved: it's no longer necessary for us to see each other twice a week, but once a week?"

"Yes."

"And did your psychiatrist say to you at a certain point, for the same reason: it's no longer necessary for us to see each other once a week, twice a month will be enough?"

"Yes."

"And did your psychiatrist say to you that you will have to meet for the rest of your life, even if only four times a year?"

"For the rest of my life? What do you mean?"

"So he doesn't envisage treating you for the rest of your life?"

"Of course not."

"When you've completely overcome your problems, you'll be able to stop seeing him, is that right?"

Martina finally turned to him, looking like a little

142

girl who wonders why adults are so stupid. She didn't answer, and he didn't insist. There was no need. He'd got what he wanted. I'd have liked to smash his face, but he'd been good.

Delissanti paused for a long time, to let the result he had obtained sink in. His face seemed expressionless. But if you looked closely, you caught a hint of something vaguely brutal and obscene.

"Is it true that once, in the course of an argument at which a number of other people – your mutual friends – were present, Professor Scianatico lost his temper and said to you, and I quote, 'You're a *compulsive liar*, you're *unbalanced*, you're *unreliable*, you're a *danger* to yourself and others'?" Delissanti's tone was different now. He hammered home the words "compulsive liar", "unbalanced", "unreliable", "danger". Anyone listening with half an ear would have had the impression of a lawyer insulting a witness. Which, when you got down to it, was precisely what Delissanti was doing. An old, cheap trick, designed to provoke the witness into losing his or her cool. Sometimes it works.

I was about to object, but at the last moment I held back. If I objected, I thought, it would be obvious I was afraid, and was thinking Martina wasn't capable of answering and getting through the cross-examination. So I stayed in my seat and said nothing. In the few seconds that passed between Delissanti's question and Martina's answer, I felt the muscles of my legs tensing and my heart beating faster. The signs of a body that's about to act by instinct and then is stopped by a command from the brain. Just like when you're about to hit someone and then a flash of reason stops you.

I was certain that Alessandra Mantovani had made the same mental journey. When I turned to her, I saw that she was shifting slightly in her seat, as if a moment earlier she had pushed herself to the edge, ready to stand up and object.

Then Martina answered. "I think so. I think he said that kind of thing to me. More than once."

"What I want to know is if you remember a specific occasion on which these things were said in the presence of mutual friends. Do you remember?"

"No, I don't remember a specific occasion. I'm sure he said things like that to me. He said a lot of other things too. For example —"

Delissanti interrupted her, in the curt, arrogant tone of someone addressing a subordinate who isn't carrying out his orders correctly. "I'm not interested in the other things, Signorina. My question is whether you remember that particular quarrel, not —"

"Your Honour, can we at least let the witness finish her answers? If counsel for the defence asks a question to understand the context in which certain words – extremely offensive words, by the way – were used, he cannot then arbitrarily limit this context to what he wants to hear, and censor the rest of the witness's story. Apart from anything else, using an unacceptably intimidating tone."

Alesssandra was still on her feet when Delissanti rose in his turn, almost shouting.

"Take care what you're saying. I won't allow a public prosecutor to address me in that tone and with such objections."

I don't know how Alessandra managed to get a word in edgeways with all that ranting and raving, but she came out with a single sentence, as short, quick and deadly as a knife thrust.

"No, Avvocato, *you* take care." She said it in a tone that froze the blood. There was a violence in those hissed words that left everyone present dumbfounded, including me.

At this point, Caldarola remembered he was the judge and that maybe he ought to intervene.

"Please calm down, all of you. I don't see the reason for this animosity and I'm asking you to stop it now. Let each person do his job and try to respect that of others. Have you any other questions, Avvocato Delissanti?"

"No, Your Honour. I take note that the witness either can't or won't recall the episode to which I refer. Professor Scianatico can tell us the story, and so, above all, can the witnesses we have indicated on our list. That is all."

"Does the public prosecutor have anything to add to her previous examination?"

"Yes, I have a couple of questions, the necessity for which has emerged as a result of the cross-examination."

Technically, it wasn't necessary for her to say that. But it was a way of underlining that this extension of the plaintiff's testimony – which was sure to be unfavourable to the defendant – was due to a mistake on the part of counsel for the defence. In other words, it wasn't a gesture of reconciliation.

"Dottoressa Fumai, would you like to tell us the other things the defendant said to you? To be more precise, the things you were about to tell us when you were interrupted."

Martina spoke about them, these other things. She spoke about the other humiliations, apart from the blows and the mental cruelty she had talked about before. Scianatico had told her she was a failure. Only one good thing had ever happened to her: she'd met him and he'd decided to take care of her. She was incapable of making decisions about her own life, and

145

so she *had* to carry out his orders and his instructions on how to behave. She had to be disciplined, and to know her place.

He'd told her she was a bitch, and bitches had to obey their masters.

She told it all, and her voice wasn't cracked or weak. But maybe it was worse. It was neutral, toneless, colourless. As if something had broken inside her again.

Caldarola adjourned for three weeks and set out a kind of schedule for the trial. At the following hearing, we would have the other witnesses for the prosecution. Then the defendant would be examined. Finally, over the course of two hearings, we would have the witnesses for the defence, including the expert witness.

I said goodbye to Alessandra Mantovani, and turned to the exit of the courtroom to follow Martina, who had left the witness stand and was just a few steps ahead of me. It was at that moment that I saw Sister Claudia. She was standing, leaning on the rail. She seemed lost in thought. Then I realized she was looking at Scianatico and Delissanti. She was looking at them in a way I'll never forget, and catching that look I thought, without having any real control over my thoughts, that this was a woman who was capable of murder.

It may seem incredible, but in the months before that afternoon, I'd found a kind of absurd equilibrium. He'd do – and make me do – those things. All I wanted was for it to end as quickly as possible. Then I'd leave the room and hide what had happened. I was a sad girl, I didn't have friends, but I had Snoopy, and my little sister, and the books I got from school and read whenever I had a free moment. I don't think my mother ever really noticed anything, until that day.

After that rainy afternoon, I don't know how, but I spoke to her. No, that's not quite right. I tried to speak to her. I don't remember what I said exactly. I'm sure I didn't tell her everything that had happened. I think I was trying to see if I could speak to her, if she was prepared to listen to me – if she was prepared to help me.

She wasn't.

As soon as she realized what I was talking about she got very angry. I was making up horrible things. I was a bad girl. Did I want to ruin our family, after all the sacrifices she'd made to keep it going? That was more or less what she said, and I didn't say any more.

A few days later, I came back from school and Snoopy wasn't there. I looked for him in the yard, I looked for him outside, in the street. I asked everyone I met if they'd seen him, but nobody knew anything. If pain exists in its purest, most desperate form, I felt it that morning. If I think again about that moment, I see a silent, washed-out scene in black and white.

That afternoon he called me into his bedroom and I didn't

go. He called me again, and I didn't go. I was in the kitchen, on a chair, my arms around my knees. With my eyes wide open, not seeing anything. I don't think there are many feelings or emotions that go together as strongly as hate and fear. Then you act one way or the other depending on which is stronger. Fear. Or hate.

He came to get me in the kitchen and dragged me to the bedroom. For the first time, I tried to resist. I don't really know what I did. Maybe I tried to kick him or punch him. Or maybe I didn't just freeze and let him do it. He was surprised, and furious. He hit me hard, as he raped me. Slaps and punches, in the face, on the head, in the ribs.

And yet – strangely – when he'd finished I didn't feel worse than the other times. Sure, I hurt all over, but I also felt a strange, fierce joy. I'd rebelled. Things would never be the same as before. He understood too, in his way.

When my mother came home she saw the bruises on my face. I looked at her without saying anything, thinking she would ask me what had happened. Thinking that now, faced with the evidence, she would believe me and help.

She turned away. She said something about making dinner, or something else she had to do.

He opened a big bottle of beer and drank it all. At the end he gave a silent, obscene belch.

27

I was lying sprawled on the sofa in my apartment, waiting for Margherita to come home and call me upstairs for dinner. I liked the fact that, even though we were more or less living together, going up to her place in the evening was like being invited out. Even though it just meant walking up two floors. It made things less obvious. Not predictable.

I was listening to *Transformer* by Lou Reed. The album that includes "Walk on the Wild Side".

Not a CD, but a genuine, original vinyl LP. With lots of crackles and pops.

I'd bought it that afternoon, in my so-called lunch break. Whenever I had a lot to do, for example when I had an appointment early in the afternoon, I didn't go back home for lunch. I'd go to one of the bars in the centre, where the bank clerks eat, and have a roll and a beer standing up. Then I'd take advantage of the break to visit a bookshop or record shop that didn't close for lunch.

That afternoon I'd ended up in a little shop run by a young man who played bass in a band: they played a kind of jazz rock, and were actually quite good. I'd heard them play several times, in the kinds of places I went to at night. The kinds of places where, in the last few years, I'd started to get the nasty feeling I was out of place.

Playing jazz rock, or whatever it was, didn't provide much of a living, though, especially as he and his band refused to play at weddings. So he sold records, though the hours he kept were very personal. There were days when he stayed closed without warning, others when he opened about eleven in the morning and stayed open without interruption until night time, when the place attracted some very strange, surreal people. The kind who made you wonder where they hid themselves during the day.

Apart from new CDs, the shop also stocked a lot of old vinyl LPs, strictly second, third or fourth hand. That morning, on the LP shelf, I found an original American copy of *Transformer*, sealed in plastic. It was a record I'd never owned, though I'd had various cassettes with a few of the songs from it, and had lost or destroyed all of them.

I'm one of the few people who still own a turntable in perfect working order, and I didn't think I should let this record go. When I got to the cash desk – or rather when I got to the chair where the bass player was sitting reading *Il mucchio selvaggio* – and heard the price, I thought maybe I could let it go after all, buy a remastered version, and with what I had left over have a meal in a luxury restaurant.

A throwback to my teenage years, when I didn't have any money. Now I earned much more than I knew what to do with. So – without the bassist/cashier being remotely aware of this interior monologue – I took out the money, paid, got him to give me a bag, insisting on a used one, put in old Lou with his Frankenstein face, and left.

I'd played the record through once, and was about to start the turntable again, put the needle back down and listen a second time, when Margherita called me and told me I could come up, she was prepared to feed me again tonight.

She'd made beans and endives, in the old way, the country way. Bean purée, wild endives, red onions from Acquaviva, hard bread and, on a separate plate, fried peppers. The peasant my parents bought fruit, vegetables and fresh eggs from when I was a child would have said this was a real luxury.

For me, there was also a bottle of Aglianico del Vulture.

Only for me. Margherita doesn't drink wine, or any alcohol. She'd been an alcoholic for many years before I met her, then she'd recovered and now she has no problem if someone drinks in her presence. "In ten days I have my first jump. Weather permitting."

She'd really gone and done the parachute course. She'd finished the theory and the physical preparation, and now she was getting ready to throw herself into empty space from a height of thirteen to sixteen hundred feet. While she talked, I tried to imagine it, and felt something like a hand clutching me in the pit of my stomach.

She was still talking, but her voice grew distant, while my mind went whirling back to a spring afternoon many years before.

There are three little boys on the sun roof of an eight-storey building. Surrounding this sun roof is a low parapet, and around that a ledge, more than three feet wide, almost like a footpath. Beyond that footpath, empty space. Terrible in its banality, with cats and shabby plants in the yard below.

One of the boys – the one who's best at football, has already smoked a few cigarettes, and can explain to the others what their willies are really for, apart from peeing – suggests a contest to test their courage.

He challenges the other two to climb over the parapet and walk along the ledge all the way round the edge of the roof. He doesn't just say it, he does it. He climbs over and starts walking fast, all the way round, and climbs back over to safety. Then the second boy tries. He takes the first steps hesitantly, then he too walks quickly and before long he too has finished.

Now it's the third boy's turn. He's afraid, but not that much. He doesn't really fancy walking so close to empty space, but it doesn't seem too dangerous to him. The other two have done it with no problems and so he can do it too, he thinks. As long as he keeps close to the parapet, just to be on the safe side.

So he climbs over too, a little clumsily – he's not very agile, certainly less so than the others – and starts to walk, looking at his two companions. He walks, running his hand along the inside of the parapet, as if for support. The one who's good at football and knows all about the use of the willy, and so on, says that's cheating. He has to take his hand away and walk in the middle of the ledge, not leaning over, as he's doing. If not, it's cheating, he repeats.

So the boy takes his hand away, shifts a few inches closer to the edge, and takes a few steps. Short steps, looking at his feet. But looking at his feet he can't help his eyes moving until they focus on a point all the way down there in the yard. It's less than a hundred feet, but it's like an abyss that can suck everything in. Where everything must *end*.

The boy looks away and tries to move forward. But now the abyss has entered into him. At that precise moment, he realizes he's going to die. Maybe not just then, maybe another time, but he is going to die.

He understands what it means, with a sudden, absolute insight.

So he grips the parapet and lowers his body, until he's almost kneeling. As if to present less surface to the

152

wind – in fact it's only a light breeze – which might make him lose his balance.

Now he's almost hunched over that low wall with his back to the abyss, and he doesn't have the courage to stand up again, not even enough to climb back over to the other side, and safety.

His two friends are saying something, but he can't hear them – or rather, he can't understand what they're saying. But suddenly he starts to feel afraid of something else. That they'll come closer and play a joke on him, like making a gesture as if to push him, or climbing over again themselves to play some terrifying game.

So he says *Help me, Mummy*, he says it under his breath, and he feels as if he wants to cry, very loud. Then, starting from his hunched position, he slowly clambers over the parapet, almost crawling, scratching his hands, grazing his knees and all that. If he stood up it would be easy to climb over, but he *can't* stand up, he can't run the risk of looking down again.

Finally he's back on the other side. The other two tease him and he lies, he tells them that as he was walking he twisted his ankle and that's why he couldn't go on, that's why he climbed over in that ridiculous manner, like a cripple. And then when they leave – and even in the days that follow – he makes sure he limps, to convince them the story about twisting his ankle was true, not just an excuse to hide his fear. He limps for a whole week, and repeats the story – to his two friends and to himself – so many times that in the end he himself can't tell what he made up from what really happened.

Ever since, at recurring intervals, the boy has dreamed of climbing over the railing of a terrace and jumping off. Directly and without hesitation.

Sometimes he dreams of jumping on the railing and walking along it like a kind of mad tightrope walker, certain not that he can do it, but that he'll fall at any moment – which promptly happens. At other times, he dreams about his two friends making fun of him, and then he runs to the railing, places a hand on it, and vaults over it, while they look on in amazement and alarm.

That'll teach them to make fun of me, he thinks as he wakes up, gripped by an overwhelming sadness, because his childhood is over, and because he could have been so many things. So many things he'll never be.

When I wake up, I always think that. I could have been so many things I'll never be, because I haven't had the courage to try.

Then I open – or close? – my eyes, get up, and go to face the day.

"Guido, are you listening to me?"

"Yes, yes, I'm sorry, I was a bit distracted. While you were talking I thought of something."

"What kind of thing?"

"Just something to do with work. Something I left unfinished."

"Something important?"

"No, no, something stupid."

28

A single hearing wasn't enough to get through all the other witnesses for the prosecution. The police inspector who'd been assigned to the investigation and who, among other things, had obtained Martina and Scianatico's phone records. The doctors from casualty who simply confirmed what they had written in their reports, of which they obviously didn't remember a word. A couple of girls from the community, who had escorted Martina on a few occasions, and in whom she had confided.

Martina's mother.

She was a sad, overweight, lacklustre woman. She and her daughter didn't look anything like each other. She spoke in a monotonous, lifeless voice about how Martina had returned home, the phone calls at night, the calls on the entry phone. She was careful to point out that she didn't know anything else, that she had never been present at any quarrels between her daughter and her daughter's boyfriend. That her daughter wasn't in the habit of confiding in her.

It was obvious she wasn't happy that she'd been forced to appear, and wanted to get away as quickly as possible.

While giving her evidence, she never once looked in her daughter's direction. When she was dismissed by the judge she hurried away. Without a gesture towards Martina, without even looking at her.

It took two hearings to get through these witnesses.

They were calm hearings, with no more clashes, because everyone – Alessandra, Delissanti, myself – knew perfectly well that the outcome of the trial didn't depend on any of these testimonies. They just provided the background. Basically, the trial came down to Martina's word against Scianatico's. Nobody had been present when he'd beaten her. Nobody had been present when he'd humiliated her. Nobody we could locate had been present when he'd attacked her in the street.

And nobody had been present at other things. Things Martina told me about only a few days before the hearing at which Scianatico was due to be examined. We met in my office and I asked her all kinds of questions. Including some very embarrassing ones, because I needed every bit of information I could find to prepare my cross-examination.

These other things, which came out in the course of the meeting in my office, might turn out to be very useful. If I could find a way of getting Scianatico to admit them, in court, in front of the judge.

The hearing was scheduled for 20 April. It was then that the outcome of the trial would probably be decided.

As long as it hadn't already been decided somewhere else, outside the courtroom. In rooms where I wasn't admitted.

The phone call came into my office about half past eight in the morning, just as I was about to leave for court. Maria Teresa told me there was a call from the Public Prosecutor's department, from Dottoressa Mantovani's office.

"Hello?"

"Avvocato Guerrieri?"

"Yes?"

"Assistant Prosecutor Mantovani's office. Hold the line, please, I'll pass you Dottoressa Mantovani."

I started to feel worried. Bad news. Anxiety.

"Guido, it's Alessandra Mantovani. I'm sorry I had the secretariat call you, but this isn't the best of mornings. I'm on call and all sorts of things are happening."

"Don't worry, what's going on?"

"I wanted to talk to you for five minutes, so if you're coming to court today maybe you could drop by."

"I can be there in fifteen minutes."

"I'll be waiting."

As I left my office and walked towards the courts and then along the corridors thick with the smell of papers and humanity, I felt my anxiety growing. The kind of anxiety you feel about things that are out of your control. An unpleasant, limp sensation, situated, for some reason, on the right-hand side of my abdomen.

I had to wait a few minutes outside Alessandra's office. She was dealing with the carabinieri, her secretary told me in the outer room. When they came out – some of them I knew well – they were carrying sheets of paper, and their faces were tense, as if they were ready for action. I was certain they were off to arrest someone.

I entered the room just as Alessandra was lighting a cigarette. On the desk was a newly opened packet of Camels.

"I didn't know you smoked."

"I quit . . . I mean I did quit six years ago," she said, taking a greedy drag. I felt almost dizzy with the desire to take one myself and the effort of resisting. If she'd offered me one I'd have accepted, but she didn't.

"Two months ago a request came in from the Senior

157

Board of the Judiciary. Asking me if I would agree to being assigned to the Public Prosecutor's department in Palermo." Another drag, almost violent.

"This isn't a good time for me. At work and especially outside. If I were inclined to dramatize, I'd say I can't go on. But I don't want to inflict my problems on you. If I wanted to unburden myself, I could write a letter to a women's magazine – using a false name obviously. You know the kind of thing: forty-year-old woman in such and such a career, life an emotional desert, burned all her bridges, growing realization that she'll never be a mother, etc, etc."

What a strange sensation. Alessandra Mantovani had always given me an impression of invulnerability. Now, suddenly, here she was, a normal woman, looking with alarm at the passing years, and the years to come, and trying desperately not to go to pieces.

"I'm sorry. I didn't call you to cry on your shoulder."

I made a gesture as if to say, no problem, if she wanted to cry on my shoulder, or whatever, she could. She didn't even see the gesture.

"I told them I agreed to the assignment. Almost without thinking. Because right now I don't know what to do. I don't know what I want ... Anyway, it's OK. I told them I was available and yesterday morning this arrived."

She handed me a fax. The letterhead was in somewhat antiquated cursive writing. Senior Board of the Judiciary. The text said that Dottoressa Alessandra Mantovani, magistrate of the court of appeal, working as an assistant public prosecutor at the law court of Bari, had been assigned, having given her agreement, for a period of six months, renewable for further periods of six months, to the Public Prosecutor's department of Palermo. Dottoressa Mantovani had to

158

present herself to the Public Prosecutor's department of Palermo within six days of the order being communicated.

The rest was technical details. Pure jargon. I stopped reading and looked up.

"Go to Palermo." Not exactly the most intelligent sentence in my life, I thought immediately afterwards.

"I have to be there by next Monday. I wanted a change, and now I've got what I wanted."

I didn't know what to say, so I said nothing and waited. She stubbed out the filter of her cigarette in a glass ashtray. She stubbed it out much more than she needed to in order to put out the cigarette.

"There are a few trials and a few investigations I'm sorry to leave. Apart from everything else. One of them is ours, this Scianatico business. With that one and some of the others, I have the nasty feeling I'm running away."

I was about to say something, but she stopped me with a gesture. She had no desire to hear me say anything forced.

"Actually, I'm not even sure why I called you. Maybe I feel like a coward and wanted to tell you directly, in person, that I'm leaving you alone with all this hassle. You'll just have to wait and see what happens. Maybe it'll be all right, and you'll get a good man. Or a good woman. Or maybe not . . ."

"Do you think you'll stay in Palermo?"

"Who knows? The transfer, as you read, is for six months, renewable. In fact, it's always at least a year, often longer. In a year, I'll think about what to do. What's for sure is that I don't have many things to keep me here in Bari. Or anywhere else, for that matter."

I felt sad and old. I felt like someone watching time passing, someone watching other people changing, growing up for good or ill, going away. Making choices. While he stays on in the same place, doing the same things, letting chance decide for him. Watching life pass him by.

Damn it, I really wanted that Camel.

That was pretty much the end of the conversation. I told Alessandra I'd drop by her office again to say goodbye, but she said it was better to say goodbye right now. She didn't know how much time she'd be spending in her office in the next few days: preparations, and so on.

She came round her desk as I stood up. I looked straight at her, just before we embraced.

She had little red spots, and lines I'd never noticed before.

As I closed the door behind me, I saw her light another cigarette. She was looking towards the window, somewhere outside.

29

Alessandra left without our having the opportunity to see each other again. As she had foreseen.

It was almost spring. Life was going on as normal. Whatever the word normal meant. Margherita and I would go out together, sometimes with her friends. Never with my friends. Even supposing I still had any.

After Emilio's funeral, I'd occasionally had the idea of calling someone and saying, *Let's go out one evening, grab a couple of beers, have a bit of a chat about life*. Then, fortunately, I'd let it go.

Two or three times, Margherita asked me if something was wrong, and if I wanted to talk. I said no thanks, not at the moment. When the right moment might be wasn't clear. She didn't insist. She's an expert on aikido and knows perfectly well that you can't push – or help – someone to do something they haven't initiated themselves.

More and more frequently I slept in my own apartment.

One time when I'd stayed with her, I was lying on the bed when I had a strange sensation. I half closed my eyes and suddenly found myself observing the scene from a different position, not the one I was in physically. I could even see myself. I was a spectator.

Margherita was getting undressed, the light was dim, everything was silent, I was lying on the bed with my eyes half closed, but I wasn't asleep.

It was a very sad scene, like one of Hopper's silent interiors.

So I got up and dressed. I said I needed to get a bit of air, and was going for a walk. Margherita looked at me and for the first time I had the feeling she was really worried about me.

About us.

She stayed like that for a few seconds, and there was a kind of sad awareness in her eyes, a fragility she didn't usually have. She seemed to be about to say something, but in the end she didn't. All she said was, *Good night*, and I escaped.

When I was at last in the street, I felt a bit better. The air was cool, almost cold, and dry. The streets were deserted. As you'd except about midnight on a Wednesday, in that part of the city.

Without thinking about it, almost without realizing what I was doing, I phoned Sister Claudia. As I dialled the number, I told myself that if she was asleep, her mobile was sure to be switched off. If she wasn't asleep . . .

She answered at the second ring. Her voice sounded a tiny bit puzzled, but she didn't ask me what had happened, or why I was phoning her at that hour. It was a good thing she didn't ask me, because I wouldn't have known what to reply.

I was walking round the city, alone. I wasn't sleepy. Maybe I'd like her to walk with me for a while and chat? Yes, I'd like that. No, there was no need for me to go and pick her up, we could meet somewhere. How about the end of the Corso Vittorio Emmanuele, in front of the ruins of the Teatro Margherita? Yes, that'd be fine. In half an hour. Half an hour. Bye. Click.

To kill that half-hour, I went to an all-night bar. A kind of splash of light in the darkness, rather squalid and unreal, in the border zone between the new town and the Libertà neighbourhood. It was a bar that had always stayed open all night, since long before the city filled up with all kinds of venues and there was an embarrassment of choice when it came to staying out late. When I was a child that bar was always full, because it was one of the few places you could go in the middle of the night, when you were out fooling around, and get a coffee, or buy unlicensed cigarettes. Now it's almost always deserted, because you can get a coffee anywhere and there are automatic cigarette machines.

I went in. The place was empty except for one couple. They were middle-aged, in other words, just a few years older than me. They were at one end of the L-shaped counter, on the shorter side of the L. I sat down on a stool, on the other side, turning my back on the big window and the street. The man was wearing a jacket and tie. He was smoking, and talking to the thin, fair-haired barman, who wore a white jacket and cap. The woman, a sad-looking, scruffily made-up red-head with deep-set eyes, was staring into the distance and seemed to be asking herself what she had done to be reduced to this.

I ordered a coffee, though I really didn't need it, because I wasn't going to get any sleep that night anyway. During the ten minutes I was there, no other customers came in. I couldn't shake off the disturbing feeling I'd already lived through – already *witnessed* – this scene.

Claudia got out of the van with the usual sinuous movement. She was dressed as usual – jeans, white T-shirt, leather jacket – but she had her hair loose, not

163

gathered in a ponytail like all the other times I'd seen her.

She nodded in greeting and I returned her nod. Without saying anything we walked along the seafront, in the light of the old iron street lamps.

"I don't know why I phoned you."

"Maybe you felt lonely."

"Is that a valid reason?"

"One of the few."

"Why did you become a nun?"

"Why did you become a lawyer?"

"I didn't know what else to do. Or if I did know, I was afraid of trying."

She seemed surprised that I'd answered, and she appeared to be considering my answer. Then she shook her head and didn't say anything. For some minutes, we walked in silence.

"Do you live alone?"

I had the impulse to say yes, and immediately felt ashamed.

"No. That is, I have my own apartment, but I live with someone."

"You mean, a woman."

"Yes, yes, a woman."

"And you don't have anything to say about the fact that you've come out alone in the middle of the night?"

As Claudia asked me the question, the faces of Margherita and my ex-wife, Sara, were superimposed in my head. It made me feel dizzy: I mean, really dizzy, as if I were somewhere high up, without any parapet, without anything to grab hold of, as if I were about to fall into empty space and everything would break into pieces, irreparably.

Then the two faces separated and returned to their

places, in my head. Whatever those places were. I hadn't answered Claudia's question, and she didn't insist.

We started walking more quickly, as if we had a destination, or something specific to do. We stopped at the end of the seafront, on the southern outskirts of the city, and sat down next to each other on the low wall of chalky stone just a couple of yards from the water.

You shouldn't be here, I thought, feeling the contact of her muscular leg on mine, and smelling her slight, somewhat bitter smell. Too close.

Everything seems out of place and once again I don't understand what's happening, I thought, as our hands – my right hand and her left – touched in an innocuous and totally forbidden manner. We both stared in front of us. As if there were something to look at between the ugly apartment blocks, standing there in the darkness, blurry against the background of the grim, disreputable suburb of Iapigia.

We stayed like that for a long time, without ever looking directly at each other. It seemed to me, without her having said or done anything, that a current of pure pain flowed from her hand.

"There's a record," she said, turning to me without warning, "that I've often listened to over the years. I'm not sure it does me good to listen to it. But I do it all the same."

I turned too. "What record?"

"*Out of Time* by REM. Do you know it?"

Of course I know it. Who do you think you're talking to, sister?

I didn't say that. I just nodded, yes, I know it.

"There's a song . . ."

" 'Losing my religion'."

She screwed up her eyes, then said yes. "You know what that means: *losing my religion?*"

"I know what it means literally. Is there another meaning?"

"It's an idiomatic expression. It means something like: I can't take it any more."

I looked at her in amazement. That was the last thing I would have expected to hear from her. I was still looking at her, without knowing what to say, when her face came closer, and then closer, until I could no longer make out the features.

I just had time to think that her mouth was hard and soft at the same time, that her tongue reminded me of when I was fourteen and kissed girls my own age, I just had time to place my hand on her back, and to feel muscles as thick as metal cables.

Then she drew back abruptly, though she kept her wide-open eyes on my face for a few seconds. Then she stood up, without saying anything, and started walking back in the direction from which we'd come. I walked behind her, and fifteen minutes later we were again at her van.

"I'm not much of a talker."

"It's not essential."

"But sometimes you just want to talk."

I nodded. You often want to talk. The problem is finding someone to listen to you.

"I'd like to talk to you another time. I mean: no flirting or anything like that. I don't know why, but I'd like to tell you a story."

I made a gesture that meant, more or less: if you like, you can tell it to me now.

"No, not now. Not tonight."

After a brief hesitation, she gave me a quick kiss. On the cheek, very close to the mouth. Before I could say anything else she was already in the van, and driving away into the night.

I walked slowly back home, choosing the darkest, most deserted streets. I felt absurdly light-headed.

Before I went to bed, I searched through my discs. *Out of Time* was there, so I put it in the player and pressed the skip button to the second track: "Losing my religion".

I listened to it with the booklet of lyrics in my hand, because I wanted to try to understand.

> *That's me in the corner*
> *That's me in the spotlight*
> *Losing my religion*
> *Trying to keep up with you*
> *And I don't know if I can do it*
> *Oh no, I've said too much*
> *I haven't said enough.*

I've said too much. I haven't said enough.

30

Honorary assistant prosecutors aren't magistrates by profession. They're lawyers – mostly young lawyers – on temporary assignment, and they're paid per hearing. Their fee is the same whether there are two or twenty cases during the hearing. Their fee is the same whether the hearing lasts twenty minutes or five hours.

As you can imagine, they generally try to get through things as quickly as possible so that they can get back to their studies.

As was to be expected, Alessandra Mantovani was replaced by an honorary assistant prosecutor. She was a recently appointed young woman I'd never seen before.

She, though, evidently knew me, because when I entered the courtroom she immediately came up to me with a very worried look on her face.

"Yesterday I had a look at the files for this hearing."

Brilliant idea, I thought. Perhaps if you'd looked at them a few days earlier you could actually have studied them. But maybe that was asking too much.

I gave her a kind of rubbery smile, but said nothing. She took our case file out of her folder, placed it on the desk, touched the cover with her index finger, and asked me if I realized who the defendant was.

"Is this Scianatico the son of *Judge* Scianatico?"

"Yes."

There was a look of alarm on her face. "How could

they have sent me to cover a case like this? For God's sake, this is only my fourth case since I was appointed. What's it all about, anyway?"

Bloody hell, didn't you tell me you'd looked at the files? Being an idiot isn't compulsory if you want to be a lawyer. Not yet, anyway. However, having said that, you're right. How could they have sent you to cover a case like this?

I didn't say that. I was really nice to her, explained what it was all about, told her it was Prosecutor Mantovani's case, but she'd been transferred to Palermo. Evidently, whoever had drawn up the schedule for the hearings hadn't noticed this was no ordinary hearing.

Hadn't she noticed?

As I was giving her these polite explanations, I was thinking I was in the shit. Up to my neck. We were about to play something like a Cassano Murge–Manchester United match. And my team wasn't Manchester United.

"And what exactly do I have to do today?"

"What you have to do, exactly, is examine the defendant."

"Damn it. Look, I won't do anything. You know this case really well and you can do it all. I'd only spoil things."

Well, you're right about that. Damned right.

"Or maybe we could ask for a postponement. Let's tell the judge we need a robed magistrate for this case and ask him to postpone it to another session. What do you think?"

"What's your name?"

She looked at me, puzzled. Then she told me her name was Marinella. Marinella Something-or-other, because she spoke quickly and swallowed her words.

"All right, Marinella, listen to me. Listen carefully.

You just sit there calmly in your seat. As you said before: don't do anything. This is what's going to happen. Counsel for the defence will examine the defendant. When it's your turn the judge will ask you if you have any questions, and you'll say no, thank you, you don't have any questions. None at all. Then the judge will ask me if I have any questions and I'll say yes, thank you, I have a few questions. In an hour, maybe more, it'll all be over, before you've even realized it. But don't even think about asking for postponements or anything like that."

Marinella looked at me, even more scared than before. The expression on my face, the tone in which I'd spoken, hadn't been pleasant. She nodded, looking like someone talking to a dangerous madman, someone who'd rather be somewhere else and hopes it will all be over really soon.

Caldarola took off his glasses – he was long-sighted – and looked towards Delissanti and Scianatico.

"Now then, at today's hearing, we are due to hear the examination of the defendant. Does he confirm his intention to undergo this examination?"

"Yes, Your Honour, the defendant confirms his willingness to testify."

Scianatico stood up resolutely, and within a second had covered the distance between the defence bench and the witness stand. Caldarola read out the ritual caution. Scianatico had the right not to answer, but proceedings would still follow their course. If he agreed to answer, his statements might be used against him, and so on, and so forth.

"So do you confirm that you wish to answer?"

"Yes, Your Honour."

"In that case, counsel for the defence may proceed with the examination."

The early stages of the examination were fairly tedious. Delissanti asked Scianatico to tell the court when he had met Martina, and in what circumstances, how their relationship had started, that kind of thing. Scianatico replied in an almost affable tone, as if trying to give the impression that he didn't bear a grudge against Martina, in spite of all the harm she had so unjustly done him. A role they had rehearsed over and over in Delissanti's office. For sure.

At a certain point he broke off in the middle of an answer. For a moment, I saw his eyes move towards the entrance to the courtroom, I saw him wince slightly, I saw that damnably smug expression of his crack just a little.

Martina and Claudia had arrived. They sat down behind me, and I turned and greeted them. Martina, following the instructions I had given her the day before when she had come to my office, handed me a package in such a way that nobody in the courtroom could fail to notice. In such a way that Scianatico, above all, couldn't fail to notice.

From the shape and size, it was clear the package contained a videocassette.

Delissanti was forced to repeat his last question.

"I repeat, Professor Scianatico, can you tell us when, and for what reason, your relationship with Signorina Fumai started to break down?"

"No . . . I can't pinpoint a particular moment. Little by little Martina's – that is, Signorina Fumai's behaviour changed."

"Can you tell us in what way her behaviour changed?"

"Mood swings. Increasingly sudden and increasingly frequent. Verbal attacks, alternating with bouts of

171

weeping and depression. On a couple of occasions she even tried to attack me physically. She was beside herself. I had the impression —"

"Objection, Your Honour. The defendant is about to express a personal opinion, which, as we all know, is not allowed."

Caldarola told Scianatico to avoid personal opinions and stick to the facts.

"Tell us what happened when Signorina Fumai was having one of her attacks."

"Mostly, she shouted. She said I didn't understand her problems and being with me would make her ill again."

"Excuse me if I interrupt. She said that she would become ill again? To what illness was she alluding?"

"She was alluding to her psychiatric problems."

"Go on. Continue telling us what happened during these attacks."

"As I've already said, she shouted a lot, wept hysterically, tried to hit me and . . . oh yes, then she accused me of having lovers. It wasn't true, of course. But she was jealous. Pathologically jealous."

"It isn't true," I heard Martina whispering behind my back. "The bastard. It isn't true."

". . . increasingly often, she told me I'd pay for it. Sooner or later, one way or the other."

"Was it during one of these arguments, in front of a number of mutual friends, that you used the words 'you're a compulsive liar, you're unbalanced, you're unreliable and you're a danger to yourself and others'?"

"Unfortunately, yes. I lost my temper as well. I shouldn't have said those things in front of other people. The sad thing is, they were true."

"Let's try to analyse these words, which you would

have preferred not to have said in front of other people, but which you couldn't hold back. Why did you say she was unreliable and a danger?"

"She'd have these violent tempers. On two occasions she attacked me. On others she went so far as to mutilate herself."

"Why did you tell her she was a compulsive liar?"

"She made things up. I don't like to say this, in spite of what she did to me. But she made up the most incredible stories. That time in particular, she told me she knew for a fact that I was having an affair with a lady who was there that night at our friends' house. It wasn't true, but there was no way to make her see reason. She told me she wanted to leave, I told her not to behave like a child, not to make a scene, but the situation soon degenerated."

I had to resist the temptation to turn to Martina.

"Did you ever threaten Signorina Fumai?"

"Never. Absolutely not."

"Did you ever use physical violence against her, during or after the period when you lived together?"

"Never of my own accord. It's true that on two occasions when she attacked me I had to defend myself, to stop her, try to neutralize her. Those were the two times she had to have emergency treatment. I hasten to add that I took her to hospital myself. And I took her to hospital on another occasion too. After she'd mutilated herself particularly badly. As I said, it was a habit of hers."

"Could you tell us exactly what form this self-mutilation took?"

"I can't remember exactly. Certainly when she lost her temper during arguments, because she couldn't get her own way, she'd slap herself, even punch herself in the face."

173

"After you stopped living together, did you have any contact with Signorina Fumai?"

"Yes. I called her many times on the phone. A couple of times I also tried to speak to her in person."

"On these occasions, either on the phone or in person, did you ever threaten Signorina Fumai?"

"Absolutely not. I was . . . I feel embarrassed saying it, but the thing is, I was still in love with her. I was trying to convince her that we should get back together. Apart from anything else, I was very worried that her mental condition might deteriorate and she might do something rash. I mean self-mutilation or worse. I thought that if we could get back together we might be able to patch things up and help her to solve her problems."

It was a moving story. A real tear-jerker. The son of a bitch should have been an actor.

"In conclusion, Professor Scianatico, you are aware of the charges against you. Did you in fact commit any of the acts attributed to you in those charges?"

Before answering, Scianatico gave a kind of bitter smile. A smile that meant, more or less, that people and the world in general were bad and ungrateful. That was why he was here, being tried unjustly for things he had not done. But he was a good person, so he didn't feel any resentment towards the person responsible. Who, apart from anything else, was a poor unbalanced woman.

"As I've said, we had two small fights during the time we were living together. Apart from that, as I've also said, I did make a lot of phone calls, some of them at night, to try to convince her that we should get back together. As for everything else, no, of course not. None of it is true."

Of course not. He couldn't deny the phone calls,

because there were records. The madwoman had made up the rest out of her destructive delusions.

That was the end of the examination. The judge told the public prosecutor that she could proceed with the cross-examination. Marinella Something-or-other, obeying my instructions, said, No, thank you, she had no questions. From the tone of her voice and the look on her face, you'd have thought the judge had asked her, "Excuse me, do you have AIDS?"

"Do you have any questions, Avvocato Guerrieri?"

"Yes, Your Honour, thank you. May I proceed?"

He nodded. He also knew that this was where the hassles started. And he didn't like hassles. Tough luck for you, I thought.

No point in leading up to things in a roundabout way, not with this case. So I got straight to the point.

"Am I correct in saying that you made a photocopy of Dottoressa Fumai's medical records during the time you lived together?"

"That's correct. I made a photocopy because —"

"Could you tell us exactly when you made this copy, if you recall?"

"You mean the day, the month?"

"I mean the period, roughly speaking. If you can also recall the day . . ."

"I can't give you an exact answer. I'm pretty sure it wasn't early on during the time we lived together."

"Did you ask Dottoressa Fumai's permission to make these photocopies?"

"Look, my intention —"

"Did you ask her permission?"

"I wanted —"

"Did you ask her permission?"

"No."

"Did you subsequently inform Dottoressa Fumai that

you had made a copy of her private records without her knowing it?"

"I didn't inform her because I was worried and I wanted to show these records to a psychiatrist friend of mine. So that we could both see exactly what Martina's problems were and how we could help her."

"To recap, then. You made this copy without asking Dottoressa Fumai's permission, in other words, secretly. And you didn't subsequently inform her that you'd done it. Is that correct?"

"It was for her own good."

"In other words, *for Dottoressa Fumai's good*, you were prepared to do things without her knowing it, invading her private space without permission."

"Objection, Your Honour," Delissanti said. "That isn't a question, it's a conclusion. Inadmissible."

"Avvocato Guerrieri," Caldarola said, "please keep your conclusions for your closing speech."

"With all due respect, Your Honour, I consider this a genuine question, regarding what the defendant *was prepared to do* according to his own quite subjective idea of what was for Dottoressa Fumai's good. But I'll happily withdraw and move on to another question. Did Dottoressa Fumai tell you herself where she kept her medical records?"

"I don't understand the question."

"Did Dottoressa Fumai tell you, 'Look, the copy of my medical records is in such and such a place'?"

"No. At any rate, I don't remember."

"So you had to search for these records in order to photocopy them? You were forced to *rifle* through Dottoressa Fumai's private effects. Is that correct?"

"I didn't rifle through anything. I was worried about her, so I searched for those papers to show them to a doctor."

Scianatico no longer seemed so at ease. He was losing his cool, and his image of manly, serene patience. Exactly what I wanted.

"Yes, you've already said that. Could you tell us the name of the psychiatrist to whom you showed these papers, after you had photocopied them clandestinely?"

"Objection, objection. Counsel for the plaintiff must avoid comments, and the word clandestinely is a comment."

That was Delissanti again. He was perfectly well aware that things weren't going very well. For them. I spoke before Caldarola could intervene.

"Your Honour, in my opinion the word clandestinely exactly describes the way in which these records were obtained by the defendant. However, I'm quite happy to rephrase the question because I'm not interested in getting into an argument." And because I got the result I wanted anyway, I thought.

"So, could you tell us the name of the psychiatrist?"

"In the end I didn't use the records. Our relationship quickly deteriorated and then she left. So in the end I didn't do anything with them."

"But you kept the photocopies?"

"I put them away and forgot all about them, until this . . . this business started."

There was rather a long pause. I unwrapped the package Martina had given me, and took out the video cassette and a couple of sheets of paper. For almost a minute I pretended to read what was written on these sheets. It was just a sideshow, and had nothing to do with the trial. The sheets of paper were photocopies of old notes of mine, but Scianatico didn't know that. When I thought the tension had risen enough, I looked up from the papers and resumed my questioning.

"Did you ever force Dottoressa Fumai to make a video recording of your sexual relations?"

Exactly what I had expected happened. Delissanti rose to his feet, shouting. It was inadmissible, outrageous, unprecedented, to ask such questions. What did the things that happened between consenting adults in the privacy of the bedroom have to do with this case? And so on, and so forth.

"Your Honour, will you allow me to clarify the question and its relevance?"

Caldarola nodded. For the first time since the start of the trial, he seemed annoyed with Delissanti. He'd pried into the most intimate and painful aspects of Martina's life. In order to ascertain the plaintiff's reliability, he'd said. And now he'd suddenly remembered that a couple's private life was sacrosanct.

That, more or less, was what I said. I said that if it was necessary to evaluate the plaintiff's personality, in order to be sure she was reliable, then the same requirement existed with regard to the defendant, given that he had agreed to be examined and, among other things, had made a series of defamatory and offensive statements about my client.

Caldarola allowed the question, and told Scianatico to answer. He looked at his lawyer, searching for help. He didn't find it. He shifted on his chair, which seemed to have become very uncomfortable. He was desperately wondering how I could have come into possession of that cassette. Which, he was convinced, contained an embarrassing record of his most private habits. In the end he asked me.

"Who . . . who gave you that cassette?"

"Could you please answer my question? If it isn't clear, or if you didn't hear it properly, I can repeat it."

"It was a game, something private. What has it got to do with this trial?"

"Is that an affirmative answer? You videotaped sexual relations with —"

"Yes."

"On one occasion? On several occasions?"

"It was a game. We both agreed to do it."

"On one occasion or on several occasions?"

"A few times."

I picked up the video cassette and looked at it for a few seconds, as if reading something on the label.

"Did you ever videotape sexual practices of a sado-masochistic nature?"

There was silence in the courtroom. Several seconds passed before Scianatico answered.

"I . . . I don't remember."

"I'll rephrase the question. Did you ever request or indeed perform sexual practices of a sado-masochistic nature?"

"I . . . we played games. Just games."

"Did you ever demand that Dottoressa Fumai submit to being tied up, or other practices involving sexual restraint?"

"I didn't demand. We agreed."

"So it's correct to say that the sexual practices I've mentioned did in fact occur, but you can't remember if you videotaped them or not."

"Yes."

"Your Honour, I've finished cross-examining the defendant. But I have a request to make . . ."

Delissanti leaped to his feet, in so far as his bulk allowed him.

"I object very strongly in advance to the admission of cassettes relating to the sexual practices of the defendant and the plaintiff. I still have strong reservations about the relevance of the questions put by the counsel for the plaintiff, but, be that as it may, the fact that certain practices occurred has now been admitted. So there is no need for pornographic material to be admitted in evidence."

Exactly what I wanted to hear him say. It had been admitted that certain practices had occurred. Precisely. They had swallowed the bait, both of them.

"Your Honour, the objection is unnecessary. I had no intention of asking for this or any other cassette to be admitted in evidence. As counsel for the defence has rightly said, the fact that certain practices occurred has been admitted. My request is quite different. In the introductory phase of the trial, counsel for the defence requested – and you, Your Honour, granted the request – that an expert witness be allowed to give evidence of a psychiatric nature about the plaintiff, with the purpose of ascertaining her reliability in relation to an overall picture of her mental state. Applying the same principle, what has emerged from the cross-examination makes it necessary to perform a similar evaluation on the person of the defendant. The psychiatrist you appoint to examine the defendant will be able to tell us if the compulsive need for sexual practices of a sado-masochistic nature, and particularly those which involve restraint, are habitually connected to impulses and actions of a persecutory nature, involving the invasion of another person's private life. In other words, if both phenomena are – or can be – expressions of a compulsive need for control. Of course, I wish to make it clear that I am not suggesting any evaluation or hypothesis at the moment as to the possible psychopathological nature of these propensities."

Scianatico's face was grey. His tan had drained away,

as if the blood had stopped flowing beneath the skin. Marinella Something-or-other was paralysed.

Delisssanti took a few seconds to recover and object to my request. With pretty much the same arguments I had used to object to his. You certainly couldn't say we were inconsistent.

Caldarola seemed undecided about what to do. Outside the courtroom, in the private conversations that had almost certainly taken place, they'd told him a different story. The trial was based on nothing more than the accusations of an unbalanced madwoman against a respected professional man from a very good family. All that needed to be done was to put an end to the whole regrettable business and avoid further scandal.

Now things didn't seem so clear-cut any more and he didn't know what to do.

For about a minute, there was a strange, tense silence and then Caldarola gave his ruling.

"The judge, having heard the request of counsel for the plaintiff; having noted that the investigation accepted in the introductory phase has not yet been concluded; having noted that the request by counsel for the plaintiff bears a conceptual relation to the category as under Article 597 of the Code of Criminal Procedure; having noted that a decision on the admission of such evidence can be made only at the end of the investigation; for these reasons reserves his decision on the request for psychiatric evaluation until the outcome of the hearing and stipulates that the proceedings continue."

It was a technically correct decision. A decision about all the new requests for the admission of evidence would be made at the end of the hearing. I knew that perfectly well, but I'd made my request at that moment in order to make it absolutely clear where I wanted to go. To make it clear to the judge exactly why I was asking these questions about sexual practices and that kind of thing.

To make it clear to everyone that we had no intention of sitting there and getting slaughtered.

Delissanti didn't like this interim ruling. It left a door dangerously open to an objectionable investigation, and to a scandal that might, if possible, be even worse than the trial itself. So he tried again.

"I beg your pardon, Your Honour, but we would like you to reject this request as of now. This further defamatory sword of Damocles cannot be left hanging over the defendant's head —"

Caldarola did not let him finish. "Avvocato, I would be grateful if you did not dispute my rulings. In this instance I will decide at the end of the hearing, that is, after having heard your witnesses, including your expert witness. A psychiatrist, as it happens. I think we have finished for today, if you yourself have no further questions for the defendant."

Delissanti remained silent for a few moments, as if looking for something to say and not finding anything. An unusual situation for him. In the end he gave up and said no, he had no further questions for the defendant. Scianatico's face was unrecognizable as he rose from the witness stand and went back to his place next to his lawyer.

Caldarola fixed the next hearing for two weeks from then. At that time, he would "hear the witnesses for the defence, as well as any further requests for the admission of additional evidence in accordance with Article 507 of the Code of Criminal Procedure".

As I took off my robe, I turned to Martina and Claudia, and it was then that I became aware of how many people there were in the courtroom. On the public benches, there were at least three or four journalists.

Scianatico, Delissanti and the cortège of trainees and flunkeys left quickly and silently. Just for a few seconds, Scianatico turned towards Martina. He had a strange – very strange – look on his face, a look I couldn't decipher, even though, with those mad, staring eyes, it reminded me of a broken doll.

The journalists asked me for a statement, and I said I had no comment. I was forced to repeat that three or four times, and in the end they resigned themselves. After what they'd seen and heard today, they already had plenty to write about.

I folded the two sheets of paper containing the copies of my old notes and put them in my briefcase with the video cassette. I didn't want to run the risk of forgetting it. I'd recorded it one night years earlier, when I couldn't sleep, and I liked to watch it from time to time. It contained an old film by Pietro Germi, with a brilliant performance by Massimo Girotti. A great film, hard to find these days.

In the Name of the Law.

After that afternoon I didn't have to go to the bedroom many more times.

It was as if he'd lost interest. I don't know if it was because I always resisted him now, or because I'd grown and wasn't a little girl any more. Or more likely both.

Whatever the reason, at a certain point he gave up.

And then I noticed the way he looked at my sister.

I was filled with anxiety. I didn't know what to do, who to talk to. I was sure that soon, very soon, he'd call her into the bedroom.

I stopped going into the yard unless Anna came down with me. If she said she wanted to stay at home reading a comic book or watching TV, I stayed with her. I stayed really close to her. With my nerves on edge, waiting to hear that voice, thick with cigarettes and beer, calling. Not knowing what I would do when it came.

I didn't have to wait long. It happened one morning, the first day of the Easter holidays. The Thursday before Good Friday. Our mother was out, at work.

"Anna."

"What do you want, Daddy?"

"Come here a minute, I have something to tell you."

Anna stood up from the chair in the kitchen, where we both were. She put the two dolls she'd been playing with down on the table and walked towards the small, narrow, dark corridor, at the end of which was the bedroom.

"Wait a minute," I said.

184

31

I've often thought about that day in court, and what happened later. I've often wondered if things could have gone differently, and to what extent it was all down to me, my behaviour at the trial, the way I questioned Scianatico.

I've never found the right answer, and it may well be better that way.

There were several witnesses, and they all told more less the same story. Which doesn't often happen. I spoke personally to some of these witnesses. In the case of the others, I read the statements they'd made at police headquarters, in the hours immediately after the events.

Martina was coming back from work – it was five-thirty or a little later – and had parked less than fifty yards from the front entrance of her mother's apartment building.

He'd been waiting for her for at least an hour, according to the owner of a clothes shop on the other side of the street, who'd noticed him because "there was something strange about his behaviour, the way he moved".

When she saw him she stopped for a moment. Maybe she thought she'd cross to the other side and get away. But then she continued walking towards him. She seemed determined, the shop owner said.

She had decided to confront him. She didn't want to run away. Not any more.

They spoke briefly, getting more and excited. They both raised their voices, especially her. She shouted at him to go away and leave her alone once and for all. Immediately after, there was a kind of scuffle. Scianatico hit her several times, slapping her and punching her. She fell, maybe she lost consciousness, and he dragged her bodily into the entrance hall.

Tancredi's phone call came while I was talking to an important client. A major entrepreneur being investigated by the tax authorities for a series of frauds, who was scared stiff at the thought that he might be arrested. One of those clients who paid on time and paid well, because they had a lot to lose.

I told him I had a major emergency on, and asked him to excuse me: we'd see each other tomorrow, or rather no, better make it the day after tomorrow, sorry again, I have to go, goodbye. When I left my office he was still there, standing in front of the desk. Looking like someone who doesn't understand, I suppose. And wondering if it might be a good idea to change lawyers.

As I was hurrying to Martina's, which was fifteen minutes from my office at normal walking pace, I phoned Claudia. I don't remember exactly what I said as I ran, breathless. But I do remember that she hung up while I was still talking, just as soon as she understood *what* I was talking about.

By the time I got there, there was a tremendous commotion. Outside the crush barriers, a crowd of onlookers. Inside them, a lot of uniformed policemen and a few carabinieri. Men and women in plain clothes, with the gold badges of the investigative police on their belts or jackets or hanging round their necks like medallions. Some of them had pistols tucked into their belts, at the front. Others were holding them in their hands, pointed downwards, as if they might have to use them at any moment. A couple of them were holding bulletproof vests, which hung like half-empty bags. They looked as if they might be about to put them on at any moment.

I asked Tancredi who was in charge of operations – assuming you could talk about operations or anyone being in charge, in all that confusion. He pointed to a nondescript man in a jacket and tie, who was holding a megaphone in his hand but didn't seem to me to know what to do with it exactly.

"He's the deputy head of the Flying Squad. It would have been better if he'd stayed at home, but the chief is abroad, so, in practice, we have to get on with it ourselves. We also called the assistant prosecutor on duty and he told us he was a magistrate, and so it was none of his business. He doesn't want to have to deal with the man, let alone decide whether or not to go in. But he's told us to keep him informed. A lot of help that bastard is, eh?"

"Have you managed to talk to Scianatico?"

"On the landline, yes. I talked to him. He said he's armed, and we shouldn't try to go any closer. I'm not really sure it's true – that he's armed, I mean. But I wouldn't like to bet on it."

Tancredi hesitated for a few moments.

"I didn't like the sound of his voice. Especially when I asked him if he'd let me talk to her. I said maybe he could just let her say hello to me and he said no, she *couldn't* right now. His voice sounded quite unpleasant, and immediately after that he hung up."

"Unpleasant in what way?"

"It's hard to explain. Cracked, as if it might break at any moment."

"Where's Martina's mother?"

"We don't know. I mean, we don't think she's at home. I asked him if her mother was there and he said no. But where she is we don't know. She probably went out to do some shopping or whatever; she'll be back any moment now and get the shock of her life. We also tried to find his father, the judge, to get him to come and talk to that fucking madman of a son of his. We managed to contact him, but he's in Rome for a conference. The Rome Flying Squad sent a car to pick him up and drive him to the airport to catch the first plane. But the earliest he can be here is in five hours. Let's hope by then we don't need him any more."

"What do you think? What should we do?"

Tancredi lowered his head and pursed his lips. As if he was searching for an answer. Or rather, as if he had an answer ready but didn't like it and was looking for an alternative.

"I don't know," he said at last, looking up. "This kind of situation is unpredictable. To decide on a strategy, you need to understand what the son of a bitch wants, in other words, what his real motivation is."

"And in this case?"

"I don't know. The only thing I'm thinking, I don't like at all."

I was about to ask him what it was he was thinking that he didn't like at all, when I saw Claudia's van arrive. In chronological order: a squeal of tyres as she came round the corner, the noise of gears suddenly changing, the back wheels mounting the pavement, the bumpers hitting a rubbish bin. She made her way through the crowd, in our direction. A uniformed policeman told her she couldn't go beyond the crush barrier which demarcated the area of operations. She brushed him aside without saying a word. He tried to block her way, but just then Tancredi ran up and told him to let her pass.

"Where are they?"

"He's barricaded himself in Martina's apartment," Tancredi said. "He's probably armed, or at least he says he is."

"How is she?"

"We don't know. We haven't managed to talk to her. He was waiting for her outside the building. When she arrived they talked for a few seconds, then she shouted something like, 'Go away or I'll call the police, or my lawyer', or both. It was then that he hit her, several times. She seems to have lost consciousness, or to have been stunned, because they saw him dragging her inside, holding her from behind, under the armpits. Someone called 113, a patrol car arrived immediately, and a few minutes later we got here."

"And now?"

"Now I don't know. In a couple of hours the special forces should arrive from Rome, and then someone will have to take responsibility for authorizing them to go in. In a case like this, nobody knows what to do. I mean if it has to be a judge, the head of the Flying Squad, the chief of police or who. The alternative would be to try and negotiate. Easier said than done. Who's going to talk to that madman?"

"I'll talk to him," Claudia said. "Phone him, Carmelo, and let me talk to him. I'll ask him if he'll let me in to see how Martina is. I'm a woman, a nun. I'm not saying he'll trust me, but he may be less suspicious than with one of you." Her tone of voice was strange.

189

Strangely calm, in contrast to her face, which was distraught.

Tancredi looked at me as if he was seeking my opinion, but without asking me anything. I shrugged my shoulders.

"I have to ask *him*," he said at last, nodding towards the deputy head of the Flying Squad, who was still wandering around with that useless megaphone in his hand. He went up to him and they talked for a few minutes. Then they both walked towards us and it was the deputy head who spoke first.

"Are you the nun?" he said, turning to Claudia.

No, I'm the nun. Don't you see my veil, idiot?

Claudia nodded.

"Do you want to try and talk to him?"

"Yes, I want to talk to him and ask him if he'll let me in. It could work. He knows me. He might trust me and if I go in I think I can persuade him. He knows me well."

What was she talking about? They didn't know each other at all. They'd never talked to each other. I turned to look at her, with a questioning look on my face. She returned my gaze for no more than a couple of seconds. Her eyes were saying, "Don't open your mouth: don't even think about it." Meanwhile, the deputy head of the Flying Squad was saying it was worth a try. At least they had nothing to lose with a phone call.

Tancredi took out his mobile, pressed the redial button and waited, with the phone flat against his ear. In the end Scianatico answered.

"This is Inspector Tancredi again. There's someone here who wants to talk to you. Can I pass her to you? No, it's not a policewoman, it's a nun. Yes, of course. We're not even thinking of coming any closer. All right, I'll pass her to you."

190

Yes, this was Sister Claudia, Martina's friend. She'd been wanting to talk to him for a long time, she had a lot of important things to say to him. Before continuing, could she say hello to Martina? Oh, she wasn't feeling well. On Claudia's face a kind of fissure opened up, but her voice didn't change, it remained steady and calm. Never mind, I'll talk to her later, if that's OK with you, of course. I think Martina wants to get back together with you. She's often told me that, even though she didn't know how to get out of the weird situation you were both in. I can't hear you very well. I said I can't hear you very well, it must be this mobile. What do you say I come up and we have a little talk? On my own, of course. I'm a woman, a nun, you have nothing to worry about. Besides, I don't like the police either. So shall I come up? Of course, you just look through the spyhole, that way you can be sure I don't have anyone with me. But in any case you have my word, you can trust me. Do you think a nun walks around with a gun? OK, I'm coming up now. On my own, of course, we agreed. Bye for now.

Apart from the things she said, what almost hypnotized me was her tone of voice. Calm, reassuring – hypnotic, in fact.

"Do you want to put on a bulletproof vest?" Tancredi asked. She looked at him without even replying.

"OK. Before you go up, I'll call you on the mobile, and you answer straight away and then leave the line open. That way at least we can hear what you're saying and we'll know what's happening."

He turned to two guys in their thirties, who looked like housing-estate drug dealers. Two officers from his squad.

"Cassano, Loiacono, you two come with me. We'll

191

go up together and stay on the stairs, just below the landing."

"I'm going with you," I heard myself saying, as if my voice had a will of its own.

"Don't talk bullshit, Guido. You're a lawyer, you do your job and let us get on with ours."

"Wait, wait. If Claudia can get the negotiation started, I could go in after her, I could help her. He knows me, I'm Martina's lawyer. I can tell him some nonsense – we'll call off the trial, withdraw the charges, that kind of thing. I can be of help, if the negotiation goes ahead. If on the other hand you have to go in, obviously I'll get out of the way."

The deputy head of the Flying Squad said that in his opinion it might work. The important thing was to be careful. Great advice. He didn't give any indication that he might come too. To avoid a bottle-neck, I presume. His ideal policeman wasn't Dirty Harry.

In my memory, what happened next is like a black-and-white film shot through a dirty lens and edited by a madman. And yet vivid, so vivid I can't tell it in the past tense.

The three policemen are in front of me, on the last flight of stairs before the landing. As far as we can get without running the risk of being seen. We are very close, almost on top of each other. I can smell the pungent sweat of the taller one: Loiacono maybe, or maybe Cassano. The doorbell makes a strange, out-of-time noise. A kind of *ding dang dong*, with an old-fashioned echo that's quite unsettling. There's a voice from inside the apartment, and Claudia says something in reply. Then silence, a long silence. I assume he's looking through the spyhole. Then a mechanical noise: locks, keys turning. Then silence again, apart from the sound of our held breaths.

Tancredi has his mobile stuck to his left ear. With his other hand he's holding his pistol, like the other two. Against his leg, the barrel pointed downwards. I remember the action all three of them performed before coming in. Slide pulled back, round in the chamber, hammer cocked gently to avoid accidental firing.

I look at Tancredi's face, trying to read in it what he can hear, what's happening. At a certain moment, the face distorts and before I need to think what it means, he cries, "Shit, all hell's breaking loose. Smash the door down, damn it, smash the door down right now."

The bigger of the two officers – Cassano, or maybe Loiacono – gets to the door first, lifts his knee almost to his chest, stretches his leg and kicks the door with the sole of his foot, at the height of the lock. There's a noise of wood splitting, but the door doesn't yield. The other policeman does exactly the same. More splitting wood, but still the door doesn't yield.

Another two, three, four very violent kicks, and it opens. We all go in together. Tancredi first, the rest of us behind. Nobody tells me to wait outside and do my job while they get on with theirs.

We pass through a number of rooms, guided by Scianatico's cries.

When we get to the kitchen, the scene that meets our eyes looks like some terrible ritual.

Claudia is sitting astride Scianatico's face: she's gripped him between her legs, keeping him immobilized, and with one hand she's pinned his throat, her fingers digging into his neck like daggers. With the other hand clenched in a fist, she's striking him repeatedly in the face. Savagely and methodically, and as I watch, I *know* she's killing him. The frame widens to include Martina. She's on the floor, near the sink. She isn't moving. She looks like a broken doll.

Cassano and Loiacono seize Claudia under her armpits and pull her off Scianatico. Once her feet are on the ground, she does what the two officers are least expecting: she attacks them so quickly they don't know what hits them, they don't even see the punches and the kicks. Tancredi takes a step back and aims the pistol at Claudia's legs.

"Don't do anything stupid, Claudia. Don't let's do anything stupid."

She's deaf to his cries and takes a couple of steps towards him. I don't think she's even seen me, even though I'm very close to her, on her left.

I don't actually make a conscious decision to do what I do. It just happens. She doesn't see me, doesn't even see my right hand as it comes towards her and strikes her on the chin, from the side. The most classic of knockout blows. You can be the strongest man in the world, but if you're hit by a good straight jab, delivered the correct way, right on the tip of your chin, there's nothing you can do. Your lights go out and that's it. It's like an anaesthetic.

Claudia falls to the floor. The two policemen are on top of her, twisting her arm behind her back and handcuffing her, with the automatic, efficient movements of people who've done it many times before. Then they do the same with Scianatico, but with him there's no need to hurry. His face is unrecognizable from all the blows, he's uttering monosyllables, and he can't move.

Tancredi goes to Martina and places his index finger

and middle finger on her neck. To see if there's still any blood circulating. But it's a mechanical gesture, a pointless one. Her eyes are staring, her face is waxen, her mouth is half open, showing her teeth, and there's a trickle of blood, already dry, from her nose. The face of death, violent death. Tancredi has seen it many times. I've seen it too, but only in photos, in the files of homicide cases. Never, until now, so concrete, so vivid, so terrifyingly banal.

Tancredi passes his hand over her eyes to close them. Then he looks around, finds a coloured dishcloth, takes it, and covers her face.

Cassano – or Loiacono – makes as if to go out and call the others, but Tancredi stops him and tells him to wait. He goes up to Claudia, who's sitting on the floor with her hands cuffed behind her back. He crouches and talks to her in a low voice for a few seconds. Finally, she nods her head.

"Take the handcuffs off."

Cassano and Loiacono look at him. The look he gives back doesn't need interpreting: it means he has no wish to repeat the order and that's it. When Claudia is once again free, Tancredi tells us all to leave the kitchen and comes out with us.

"Now listen to me carefully, because in a few seconds there'll be chaos in here."

We look at him.

"Let me tell you what happened. Claudia went in. He attacked her and a scuffle started. We heard it all over the phone, and that's when we broke in. When we got to the kitchen they were fighting. *Both of them.* We intervened, he resisted, and obviously we had to hit him. We finally managed to immobilize him and handcuff him. That's it. That's all that happened."

He pauses, and looks at us one after the other.

"Is that clear?"

Nobody says anything. What can we say? He looks at us again for a few moments and then turns to Cassano, or maybe Loiacono.

"Call the others, without making too much fuss. Don't go out shouting, there's really no need. And send in the ambulance people too. For that piece of shit."

The officer turns to go. Tancredi calls him back.

"Hey."

"Yes?"

"I don't want to see any journalists in here. Is that clear?"

By the time we left, the apartment was filling with policemen, carabinieri, doctors, nurses. The deputy head of the Flying Squad resumed command, so to speak, of the operation.

Tancredi told me to take Claudia away, make sure she calmed down, and call him again in an hour. We had to go to police headquarters for Claudia's statement, and he wanted to be the one to take it, obviously.

He wasn't looking at her as he spoke. She, on the other hand, was looking at him and it seemed as if she wanted to say something. She didn't say anything, but there was probably no need.

We walked back to her van, which was still there, squashed up against the dustbin.

"Could you drive, please?"

"Do you want to see a doctor?"

"No," she said, but her hand went unconsciously to her chin, and she took it between her thumb and the other fingers, to check it was still in one piece, after the punch. "No. It's just that I don't feel up to driving."

196

It was still light and the air was cool and mild, I thought, as I got into that old contraption, on the driver's side.

It was April, I thought.

The cruellest month.

32

We drove along all the seafronts in the city, two or three times, in Claudia's van, without saying a word. When I saw that an hour had gone by, I asked her if we could go to police headquarters. She said yes. In a toneless, colourless voice.

We drove to police headquarters, and they took her statement. Tancredi was there, along with a very pleasant young policewoman. They wrote down the story Tancredi had already told us when we were still in Martina's apartment.

It didn't take long, and Claudia signed the statement without reading it.

When I asked if they needed my statement too, Tancredi looked me in the eyes for a few moments.

"What statement? You didn't go in until it was all over. So what kind of statement do you want to make?"

Pause. I instinctively glanced at the policewoman, but she was making a photocopy and wasn't paying any attention to us.

"Just go, we've got work to do. It'll take us all night to get the paperwork ready to send to the Prosecutor's department tomorrow."

He was right. What kind of statement did I want to make?

There was nothing to add, and so Claudia and I left.

Margherita was out, at work. I was glad she wasn't in

because I had no desire to tell her what had happened. Not that evening, at least. So I didn't switch the mobile on again: I'd turned it off when we went into police headquarters.

We walked back to the van without saying a word. Claudia didn't break the silence until we were sitting. She was looking straight ahead, her face expressionless.

"I don't want to go back. I want to go for a drive."

I didn't want to go back either. I didn't want to go anywhere. I started the engine without saying anything and set off. I took the autostrada after the Bari North tollgate, drove 500 yards, and stopped at the first motorway café. Absurdly, I felt like eating. In that casual, unstructured way you eat on long journeys, which I really like. Maybe that was why I'd taken the autostrada. We had two cappuccinos and two slices of cake. Because, absurdly, Claudia was also hungry.

When I paid, I asked the cashier for a cigarette lighter and a packet of MS. The packet was soft, and I held it in my hand for a few seconds before putting it in my pocket.

We set off again, into the still, welcoming darkness of that April night.

"Do you remember there was a story I wanted to tell you?"

"Yes."

"Let's stop somewhere. Somewhere quiet."

About twelve miles further on, I pulled into a parking area, surrounded by deserted, dark, silent trees and dimly lit by a few street lamps. There was something strange and reassuring in the occasional muffled sound of a car speeding by. We got out of the van and went and sat on a bench.

White Nights came into my mind. I mean the actual words written in my head in printed characters. Along

199

with images from the film, and words from the book. A bench, two people who can't sleep, spending the night talking. Hovering in a suspended universe.

Calmly, I unwrapped the packet. First the silver thread, then the plastic at the top, then the tinfoil. I tapped the closed part with my index and middle fingers to get the cigarette out.

I closed my eyes and felt the smoke hit my lungs and the cool air on my face.

I didn't care about anything, I thought, as I smoked that harsh, strong cigarette with my eyes closed. I lost contact with reality, I was floating somewhere, which was both there, in that car park, and at the same time somewhere else. Somewhere in the distant past, somewhere dark and welcoming and forgotten.

"I'm not a nun."

I opened my eyes and turned to her. She had her elbow on her knee and her head on her elbow. She was looking – or seemed to be looking – towards the dark shadow of a eucalyptus.

She told me her story.

I opened the door and stopped just inside the room, my arms hanging at either side of my body. He raised his head and looked at me. There was a hint of surprise in those filmy eyes.

"Where's Anna?"

As I answered, I realized I was shaking all over. And I mean all over. Legs, arms, shoulders, chin.

"Leave her alone."

He craned his neck towards me and half closed his eyes, in an instinctive gesture. As if he didn't believe what he'd just heard. As if he didn't believe that I could challenge him like that.

"Tell Anna to come up here right now."

"Leave the child alone."

He got up from the bed.

"I'm going to show you, you little bitch."

I was shaking all over, but I stayed where I was, just inside the room. All I did was lift my right arm, when he was almost on top of me.

That was when he saw the knife. It was a long, sharp knife with a point. The kind that's used for cutting meat. He was so close, I could see the hairs in his nose and ears. I could smell his body and his breath.

"What the hell do you think you're doing with that knife, you whore?"

Those were his last words. I put my left hand over my right, and pushed with all the strength I had. From bottom to top, all the way. He jerked slightly and then, slowly, put his hands on mine, in a gesture of self-defence that was pointless now.

201

We stayed like that, united for an endless moment, hands and eyes locked.

His eyes were full of astonishment. Mine were empty.

Then I freed my hands, took a few steps back, without turning. And closed the door.

Anna hadn't heard a thing – he hadn't even groaned – and didn't notice anything. I took her by the hand and told her we had to go down to the yard. She took her dolls and followed me. As we were going downstairs, she stopped and pointed.

"You've hurt yourself, Angela. There's blood coming out of your hand."

"It's nothing. I'll wash it at the tap in the yard."

"But you have to put disinfectant on it."

"There's no need. Water will be fine."

After that, my memories are confused. A series of fragments, some clear, others so dark you can't see anything.

At a certain point, my mother came back, passed us and went upstairs. I don't remember if she greeted us, or just saw us. A few minutes later we heard her terrible screams. Then people leaning over the balconies, or coming down to the yard, or climbing the stairs in our block. Then noises of sirens, and flashing blue lights. Dark uniforms, a crowd pressing around our door, the hours passing, night starting to fall, people talking under their breaths while two men in white shirts carried out a stretcher with a body on it, covered in a sheet.

I stayed behind, holding my sister by the hand, until a nice lady came up to us and said we had to go with her.

We were taken to an office. There was a man there, and the lady asked us if we wanted something to eat. My sister said yes, I said no thanks, I wasn't hungry. They brought her a ham roll and a Coke, and when she'd finished eating they asked us questions. They wanted to know if anyone had come to see our daddy, if we had seen any strangers entering our block, anything like that. I asked if they could take my sister out, because I had some things to tell them. They looked at each other and then the lady took my sister by the hand and took her out of the room.

By the time she came back, I was already telling my story. I told it all, calmly, starting with that summer morning and finishing the Thursday before Good Friday.

Calmly, without feeling anything.

33

I lit my third or maybe fourth MS and gratefully felt the smoke split my lungs.

Claudia told me the rest. What happened afterwards. The years in reformatory. Her schooling. Sister Caterina, who worked there as a volunteer and came almost every day to see the boys and girls who were confined there. She was an unusual nun, different from the others. She dressed in normal clothes, she was young, she was friendly, she was determined not to talk about religion, and she befriended little Angela. The only inmate who was there for a murder, committed before her fourteenth birthday. Confined to reformatory as a security measure because she was under fourteen years of age, and couldn't be charged with a crime. And because she was dangerous.

Sister Caterina taught a lot of things to that strange, silent child, who minded her own business and didn't make friends with anyone. She brought her books, and the girl devoured them and kept asking for more. She taught her to play the guitar, she taught her to make really nice desserts. She taught her first aid, because she was a nurse.

One day, as they were chatting together in the courtyard of the reformatory, the girl, who was now a young woman, told the sister that she didn't want to be called Angela any more. She'd soon be leaving the reformatory and she wanted Sister Caterina to give her a new name. For outside. For her new life.

The sister was disturbed by this request and told the girl she would have to think about it. When she came back the next time, the first thing the girl asked her was whether she had her new name. Sister Caterina said her mother's name was Claudia. The girl said it was a beautiful name, and from now on she would be called Claudia. Sister Caterina was about to say something, but then didn't. She took off the little wooden crucifix she always wore – the only visible sign that she was a nun – and put it round the girl's neck.

When she left the reformatory, Claudia was entrusted to a family in the north, because she had said she didn't want to go back to live with her mother. She took a vocational course, gained a diploma, got a job, started practising martial arts. Karate first, then that lethal discipline invented centuries earlier by a nun.

One day, she heard they were looking for volunteers to lend a hand in a community that provided a shelter for ex-prostitutes and abused women. She applied, and at the interview she said she was a nun. Sister Claudia, from the order of Lesser Franciscans. Sister Caterina's order.

"I don't know why it came into my head to say I was a nun. I couldn't explain it even now. Maybe, unconsciously, I thought if I was a nun I'd be safe. I don't mean physically. I'd be safe from relationships with people. I'd be safe . . . from men, maybe. I thought everything would be easier, that I wouldn't have to explain a whole lot of things."

She turned to look at me, passed her hand over her face, then continued.

"I know what you're thinking. Wasn't I afraid of being found out? I don't know. The fact is, nobody ever doubted I was really a nun. It may seem strange, but that's the way it is. It's funny. Say you're a nun and nobody thinks of checking if you really are. Nobody asks for your papers. Why should a woman pretend to be a nun? People accept it and that's it. If anyone asks you how come you never wear a habit, you just say it isn't compulsory in your order, and that's the end of it. So before you know it, everyone thinks you're a nun."

Another pause. Again, she passed her hand over her darkened face.

"It felt comfortable. It was my way of hiding while still being in the middle of people. It was my way of protecting myself. It was my way of escaping, while staying in the same place."

There wasn't much else to tell. She'd started working in that community. It was part of an association that had branches all over Italy. When she heard they were planning to open a new refuge near Bari, and were looking for someone with experience to work there full time, for a small salary, to get the community started, she applied.

When she finished her story she asked me for a cigarette. I was strangely glad that she did and that I could give her one and take another one myself and we could smoke together, in silence, while from time to time the sounds of cars could be heard coming closer, passing our car park, and speeding off into the distance.

"There's a dream I have once or twice a year. He's calling little Angela from the bedroom, that summer morning. Little Angela goes in, he makes her close the door, makes her sit on the bed, and at that moment the door opens again and Sister Claudia comes in. To save the child. But she never does, because just then I always wake up."

She turned the cigarette, almost completely burned down now, between her fingers. She looked at the embers, as if they hid a secret, or an answer.

"Once I even dreamed that someone brought my dog Snoopy to the refuge. It wasn't dead, it had just run away."

She gave a kind of smile, half closing her eyes, trying to see something in the distance.

There was a catch in my throat and I had to force myself to swallow.

"You know, back in the reformatory, Sister Caterina gave me a poem to read, by a woman poet, I can't remember her name. She was English, or maybe American. It was dedicated to a mongrel, like Snoopy. It started: *If there isn't a God for you, there isn't a God for me either.*

"That's nice." As I said this, I realized they were the first words I had uttered since we'd sat down on that bench, in that service area, on that autostrada. I felt a strange sense of peace as I said it. She took my hand and held it tight, without looking at me.

But I looked at her.

She was weeping silently.

Before we got back in the van I found a litter bin and threw away the cigarettes and the lighter.

Claudia said she would drive, and she got me back home in less than an hour.

She held my hand again for a while, before she said goodbye. Outside, the night was starting to be less dark.

When I got in, the first thing I did was clean my teeth, to take away the taste of the cigarettes.

Then I opened all the windows, took out an old, rare vinyl disc and put it on the turntable.

The cool wind of dawn was blowing through the apartment, and I leaned back in the rocking chair just as the first crackly notes rang out.

Albinoni's famous adagio. Over those notes, as if coming from another dimension, the mysterious speaking voice of Jim Morrison.

34

Scianatico was arrested for kidnapping and murder. And resisting a police officer of course, since, according to the written statements, he'd tried to fight the policemen who were bursting into the apartment to arrest him.

According to the autopsy, Martina had died from a number of violent blows – punches, probably – to the head and a knock against a hard surface. A wall or the floor. The medical expert said that Martina was probably still alive when she was dragged into the building and then into the apartment.

In the trial that followed with unusual haste, Scianatico was again defended by Delissanti, who tried everything he could to have him declared incapable of understanding and free will. His expert witness mentioned a psychotic imbalance that had triggered the attack and the murder, a failure to process feelings of grief for the end of the relationship, a serious depressive syndrome when the patient realized what he had done, and a whole lot of bullshit like that. Scianatico tried to confirm the diagnosis with two highly dubious suicide attempts in prison.

But the court-appointed psychiatrist didn't buy it. He said the two suicide attempts were simulated acts and concluded his evaluation with the comment that the defendant was an individual with ". . . a compulsive need for control, a very low tolerance for frustration, a borderline personality structure, and a narcissistic disorder . . . but technically capable of understanding (in the sense of being perfectly aware of the significance of his actions) and free will (in the sense of being able to make decisions freely and to choose his own behavioural patterns)".

And so, after a three-month trial covered in relentless detail in the newspapers and on television, Scianatico was found capable of understanding and free will and was sentenced to sixteen years' imprisonment, the charge of voluntary homicide being reduced to one of manslaughter. In plain language: he went there to beat her up but didn't intend to kill her.

Technically, a correct decision, but the first thing I thought when I read the news in the papers was that the bastard would be out on day release within seven or eight years. Provided they didn't reduce his sentence at the court of appeal.

But the court of appeal didn't give him any more reductions. In such a notorious case, with so much media attention, nobody wanted to risk being accused of favouritism towards Judge Scianatico's son.

Actually, that was former Judge Scianatico's son. The old man had taken leave of absence immediately after the murder and then, without ever returning to work, retired.

Caldarola never saw our civil case through to the end. A few months after the final events he was transferred to the court of appeal, and so the trial had to start again with another judge. This time, Delissanti chose what you might call a tamer line of defence. With the murder trial in progress, it was not in their best interests to go over, yet again, the things Scianatico had done before, especially with the journalists making so much noise. It was not in their best interests to talk about the fights, the violent sex, the harassment, the stalking, or the things the murder victim had been subjected to in the months and years before she became a murder victim. So at the first hearing they calmly plea bargained and managed to get six months' imprisonment.

The disciplinary proceedings against me were shelved. There too it was in nobody's interests to go over the whys and wherefores of a case that had ended the way it had. Not even mine. The ruling, which was quite brief, said that I had not committed any disciplinary offence, but had simply "interpreted with vigour, but within the limits of ethical correctness, the mandate of counsel for the plaintiff".

Alessandra Mantovani has stayed in Palermo. When the assignment was nearly over, she asked for, and obtained, a permanent transfer. Now she works in the anti-Mafia department and every now and again I read her name, and see her photograph – her face looking tired and hardened – in some newspaper. It always gives me a curious twinge of sadness. Like the one I felt when she told me she was leaving.

Claudia, on the other hand, has stayed in Bari. She still runs the refuge but has stopped calling herself Sister. Not that she ever held a press conference or put up posters to tell everyone she wasn't a nun.

Whenever a new girl arrives in the community, she simply introduces herself with her name and that's it. If anyone who knew her before calls her "Sister", she tells them just her name will be fine. In other words, Claudia.

Which isn't the name she has on her papers, but that doesn't really matter. Her real name is Claudia. The name on her papers was given to her by her natural parents. If you can apply the word *natural* to a father who does things like that to his little girl and a mother who lets him do it, pretending she doesn't see or hear a thing.

Her real mother, her only family, had been Sister Caterina, in the reformatory.

35

When I told Margherita that I'd like to take up parachuting, she looked at me for a long time without
saying anything. "Was I trying to show her I could still
surprise her?" she asked when she got the power of
speech back. If so, I'd succeeded.

A few days later I started the course.

During those weeks I felt a very strange sensation
I'd never known before, a mixture of definite fear and
unsettling serenity. A sense of the inevitable and a
mysterious dignity.

The night before the jump, I didn't sleep a wink.
Obviously.

But I stayed in bed all night, wide awake, thinking
about many things, remembering many things. The
most vivid of all was that terrible children's game on
the ledge, so many years ago.

Every now and again a wave of absolutely pure fear
swept over me. I let it flow through my body, like a
current of energy, until it had passed. Sometimes these
waves were stronger, and lasted for a longer time.
Sometimes I thought I was going to die the next day.
Sometimes I thought I'd pull out at the last moment.
But that too passed.

If Margherita noticed I hadn't slept, she didn't say
anything in the morning.

Strangely, I didn't feel tired. On the contrary, my
arms and legs felt loose and my mind clear and clean. I
wasn't thinking about anything.

*

The deafening noise of the plane dropped until it became a kind of background rumble. Powerful but contained, in the half-light of the cockpit. The pilot had reduced speed to the minimum and it almost seemed as if the plane was suspended between the earth and the sky.

There were six of us due to jump. I and three others would go first. Then the instructor and Margherita, who had asked to be there and had told me about it only that morning.

When the hatch was thrown wide open the wind rushed in, and the light was unsettling.

I was very close to the mystery of life and death.

The instructor told me to place myself across the opening, as I had been taught. I did as I was told. A few seconds passed and he signalled to me to jump. I looked down and didn't move. It was like an endless scene in slow motion, developed frame by frame. I stood there motionless. He repeated that I should jump, but I didn't move. Everything was absurdly still.

Then Margherita came up to me, squeezed my arm and said something in my ear. I couldn't make out the words over the noise of the plane, but there was no need.

So I closed my eyes and let go.

A few seconds, or a few centuries, later I heard the *phutt* of the parachute opening. And the incredible silence of the empty sky, with the plane already a long way away.

My eyes were still closed when I became aware of a strange yet familiar noise. It took me a while to realize it was my own breath, emerging from deep inside the silence, the fall, the fear.

I still had my eyes closed when I heard my name being called. It was only then that I opened them, and saw where I was. I saw the world below me, and realized I was flying without fear. And I saw Margherita, a hundred, a hundred and thirty feet above me, waving to me.

I felt an emotion that can't be explained, and I raised my hand too.

I raised both hands, waving like I used to when I was a little child and I was very happy.

REASONABLE DOUBTS

Gianrico Carofiglio

Counsel for the defence Guido Guerrieri is asked to handle the appeal
of Fabio Paolicelli, who has been sentenced to sixteen years for drug smug-
gling. The odds are stacked against the accused: not only the
fact that he initially confessed to the crime, but also his past as a
neo-Fascist thug. It is only the intervention of Paolicelli's beautiful
half-Japanese wife that finally overcomes Guerrieri's reluctance.

Reasonable Doubts, Carofiglio's third novel featuring Guerrieri,
follows on from the critical and commercial success of
Involuntary Witness and *A Walk in the Dark*.

PRAISE FOR *REASONABLE DOUBTS*

"The role of lawyer Guido Guerrieri is to take on impossible
cases that have little chance of success. The lawyer
accepts this case only because he's fallen in lust with
the prisoner's wife; his efforts to prove his client's innocence
bring him into dangerous conflict with Mafia interests.
Everything a legal thriller should be." *The Times*

This novel is hard-boiled and sun-dried in equal parts.
Guerrieri stumbles into a case involving old enmities, a femme
fatale and a murky conspiracy. But where Philip Marlowe
would be knocking back bourbon and listening to the snap of
fist on jaw, Guerrieri prefers Sicilian wine and Leonard
Cohen... The local colour is complemented by snappy legal
procedural writing which sends the reader tumbling through
the clockwork of a tightly wound plot." *The Financial Times*

"Carofiglio, until recently an anti-Mafia prosecutor in southern
Italy, is particularly well placed to write legal thrillers, and he
does so with considerable brio, humour and skill." *The Daily Mail*

www.bitterlemonpress.com

INVOLUNTARY WITNESS

Gianrico Carofiglio

A nine-year-old boy is found murdered at the bottom of a well near a popular beach resort in southern Italy. In what looks like a hopeless case for Guido Guerrieri, counsel for the defence, a Senegalese peddler is accused of the crime. Faced with small-town racism fuelled by the recent immigration from Africa, Guido attempts to exploit the esoteric workings of the Italian courts.

More than a perfectly paced legal thriller, this relentless suspense novel transcends the genre. A powerful attack on racism, and a fascinating insight into the Italian judicial process, it is also an affectionate portrait of a deeply humane hero.

PRAISE FOR *INVOLUNTARY WITNESS*

www.bitterlemonpress.com